HARMONY

PROJECT ITOH

D0111941

HARMONY

PROJECT ITOH

TRANSLATED BY ALEXANDER O. SMITH

SAN FRANCISCO

Harmony
© 2008 Project Itoh
Originally published in Japan by Hayakawa Publishing Inc.

English translation © 2010 VIZ Media, LLC
Cover and interior design by Sam Elzway

No portion of this book may be reproduced or transmitted in any form or by any means without written permission from the copyright holders.

HAIKASORU
Published by
VIZ Media, LLC
295 Bay Street
San Francisco, CA 94133

www.haikasoru.com

Itoh, Project, 1974-2009.
 [Harmony. English]
 Harmony / Project Itoh ; translated by Alexander O. Smith.
    p. cm.
 ISBN 978-1-4215-3643-9
 I. Smith, Alexander O. II. Title.
 PL871.5.T64H3713 2010
 895.6'36--dc22
                                  2010017385

The rights of the author of the work in this publication to be so identified have been asserted in accordance with the Copyright, Designs and Patents Act 1988. A CIP catalogue record for this book is available from the British Library.

Printed in the U.S.A.
First printing, July 2010

CONTENTS

<part:number=01:title=Miss.Selfdestruct/>

```
<?Emotion-in-Text Markup Language:version=1.2:enc
oding=EMO-590378?>
<!DOCTYPE etml PUBLIC :-//WENC//DTD ETML 1.2
transitional//EN>
<etml:lang=jp>
<etml:lang=en>
<body>
```

01

I have a story to tell.

```
<declaration:calculation>
     <pls: The Story of a Failure>
     <pls: The Story of a Defector>
          <eql: In other words, me.>
</declaration>
```

02

```
<theorem:number>
     <i: When children become adults, they become data.>
     <i: When adults die, they are liquefied.>
</theorem>
```

No, that's not quite right. Better to describe it in prohibitions:

```
<rule:number>
    <i: A child's body should not be reduced to data
    until it has matured.>
    <i: When an adult dies, the body should be
    disincorporated into liquid.>
</rule>
```

Children's bodies are restless, eager. They won't sit still, not even for a moment. An adult's body is always moving too—moving steadily toward death—but at a far more deliberate pace. WatchMe doesn't belong in a restless body. WatchMe doesn't belong in the body that skips and runs. WatchMe monitors constancy, but a child grows every day. They're changing all the time. What's constant about that?

So,

```
<list:item>
    <i: While my tits are still getting bigger…>
    <i: While my ass is still getting bigger…>
    <i: No WatchMe in me!>
    <i: A body with WatchMe is an adult body.>
</list>
```

For a high school girl like me, growing up was the last thing I wanted to do.

"Let's show 'em, the both of us," Miach said one day. Miach Mihie was her full name. I sat behind her in class. While everyone was getting ready to go home, she turned around in her chair and leaned over my desk.

"We'll make a declaration, together: we'll never grow up."

```
<list:item>
    <i: our bodies>
    <i: our tits>
    <i: our pussies>
```

```
        <i: our uteruses>
    </list>
```

"These things are *ours*. That's what we'll tell them. We'll whisper it at the top of our lungs!"

Yeah, me and Miach were the weird kids.

In a world of kind, thoughtful, group-consciousness types, we might not have been *entirely* on our own, but we sure felt like it.

```
    <declaration>
        <i: We won't become them.>
    </declaration>
```

Part of a whole world practically tripping over itself not to offend others, to be thoughtful of others—even of me.

"Hey, Tuan, you know what?" Miach's eyes sparkled. Miach knew everything. Of all the delinquents in our class, she had the best grades. Miach never spoke to anyone besides me and Cian—Cian Reikado, our other friend—unless it was absolutely necessary.

I still don't know what Miach saw in us. I didn't get very good grades, and while I wasn't ugly I wasn't particularly attractive either. The same went for Cian. Sometimes I wondered why she hung out with us at all, but I never asked. Not once.

"A long time ago, there were men who would actually pay to have sex with a couple of innocent bodies like ours. So all these girls who weren't even poor would sell themselves as fuck toys, and they wouldn't even feel guilty about it at all. And neither would the morally depraved men who bought them. They'd meet up in hotels and pay them *cash*."

"What?" I said, giggling. "You want to sell your body?" The way Miach was talking, she sounded like she would be off for the nearest red-light district right then if she could—that is, had they still existed anymore. There, a little girl could be as depraved as she wanted to be. She could throw away her whole life, destroy her body with loveless sex, diseases, alcohol, recreational drugs, and cigarettes.

Plague, booze, and smokes—loot too good to pass up.

You couldn't find any of these things in Japan, a nation obsessed with health, or anywhere else under admedistration rule, for that matter. All these vices, things which had gone more or less ignored in the past, had been carved into a list of sins by the all-powerful hand of medicine, and one by one, they had been purged from society.

"If there were still men of that caliber of depravity around today, maybe growing up wouldn't be as bad as it sounds. But there aren't."

She had a point. Had the streets been filled with people secure in their own perversion, then maybe, just maybe, we wouldn't hate school and pretty much everything else so much. But the world kept getting healthier and more wholesome, more peaceful, more beautiful, and just depressingly *good*. Have a little self-respect, you might tell it, but I doubt the world would care.

```
<declaration:anger>
    <"We don't know what rock bottom is like. And they
    wouldn't let us know, even if we tried.">
</declaration>
```

Miach's favorite line.
Miach knew everything. For example:

```
<list:item>
    <i: How to tweak a medcare unit to convert
    medicules into a chemical weapon capable of
    killing a city of fifty thousand people.>
    <i: How to trick a medcare unit into making
    small amounts of feel-good endorphins.>
</list>
```

"Medcare units are these magic boxes," she told me once. "All you need is a half tank of medicules and you can do just about anything. Want to fill a bathroom with poison gas? Beyond easy."

Telling us in gory detail about the many dangers of medcare units was one of Miach's favorite things to do. Even a residential medcare unit was highly adaptable. All it had to do was download a recipe and it could throw together a compound to generate just the right kind of medicules you needed to take care of any illness. It was like a magic hand that reached in and crushed disease. To Miach the ramifications of this were obvious: flip a switch, and the medcare unit would go from good to evil, from panacea to plague. The only thing keeping people from doing it was the medcare unit telling them they couldn't. All that stands between us and Armageddon is a little bit of coding, she'd say. Turn one little routine on its head, and you could overturn the world. It all came down from the top. The admedistration checked your WatchMe data in order to download the right information to the medcare unit in your home, which would then produce the necessary substances to fight whatever was ailing you.

"Think of the billions of people in the world under constant WatchMe surveillance, consuming whatever their medcare unit pumps out. Take control of the system, and you could slam every last one of them with some nasty, incurable disease. Or worse.

"It's just a matter of wanting to do it," Miach would say.

When she wasn't talking to us, Miach would sit on a bench in a park where the local children played and quietly read books. Reading text on dead-tree media was her only hobby, as far as we could tell. I asked her once why she bothered with books when she could just call up the same thing in augmented reality on the net.

"When you want some real solitude, dead-tree media's the only way to go. Then it's just the two of us. Me and the medium," was Miach's answer. She went on in that cool, silky smooth, soporific voice of hers. "It works with movies and paintings too. But a book will give you the most persistence by far."

"What do you mean, 'persistence'?"

"The persistence of solitude."

So Miach would download the text she wanted from the Borgesnet and go to a printer who would make her an actual physical copy. Places that printed books for hobbyists weren't easy to come by, but you could still find them if you looked. The majority of Miach's spending money went to book-making, and she probably had her hobby to thank for her formidable store of knowledge.

She spent her days swimming through a sea of letters, searching for something to give her that edge she wanted.

"I have to think I'm pretty sharp by now," she was fond of saying.

I didn't need to ask what she meant.

She was honing herself to be the perfect public enemy. A vicious attack dog, dreaming of the day she could take on the whole so-stifling-sweet-it-felt-like-it-was-choking-you-with-a-silken-thread world.

"So what I'm saying is, if a few people had the inclination, they could kill everyone in Japan—" she snapped her fingers— "like that. It's just a matter of wanting to."

"But you can't just kill people," Cian would say, but her words seemed flimsy in the face of Miach's conviction. Or maybe that was just my resentment talking—resentment that I had never even thought about whether you shouldn't do such a thing, or why.

Maybe:

```
<list:item>
     <i: Because I have a father.>
     <i: Because I have a mother.>
     <i: Because I have friends.>
</list>
```

Could be. But take away the family, and the only people I could call my friends were Miach, who had suggested we make poison gas with a residential medcare unit, and Cian, who never suggested much of anything.

"There's a difference between wanting to do something and wanting to do something like *that*," I said with a grin.

Miach smiled back. "Wanting to do something *horrible,* that's right. By the time we're adults, just thinking about things like this will be a crime."

"Nobody's going to come and arrest you just for thinking something."

"I'm not talking about police. I'm talking about a crime in our hearts, our souls."

Miach reached out and grabbed one of my breasts.

My left breast. The breast closest to my heart.

My eyes went wide as Miach started squeezing my breast hard, her face serious as she spoke. Next to us, Cian sat there, gaping.

"When this breast has gotten as big as it's going to get, we'll all have WatchMe inside us."

Miach's fingers squeezed my nipple so hard I thought it would pop. She wanted me to feel the pain.

"A regiment of medicules inside you, watching you, snitching on you. Little nanoparticles turning our bodies into what? Into data. They reduce our physical state to medical terminology and hand the information, *our bodies*, over wholesale to some well-meaning admedistration bureaucrat."

"Miach, p-please!"

Ignoring me, she went on, "Could you stand that happening to you, Tuan?"

"What I can't stand is what your hand is doing to me right now!"

But Miach kept squeezing and smiling. "Do you think you could stand letting them replace your body with data? I know I couldn't."

≡

Miach first discovered me in the park.

Some parents were playing with their kids on a warped pink jungle gym, and there she was, a girl my age, sitting on a bench reading a book. I had seen her in class, so I knew who she was. Everyone knew who she was.

Spooky.

That was what they called her. A lot of the cliques in school, girls and boys alike, had approached her in the beginning—her grades alone meant she stood out—but she managed to remain unaffiliated, preferring a beautiful kind of solitude.

Some of the groups misunderstood and took pity on her. Not that I blamed them for not getting Miach. Everyone was so concerned about everyone else as it was. And with goodwill toward men the norm of the day, it was hard to imagine anyone who didn't want to take part in all that. So the girls would invite her over to eat lunch with them, or want to text with her, all trying to get her attention.

We were taught to be kind to one another, to support one another, to live in harmony. That was what it meant to be adult, they said.

```
<list:item>
    <i: Love thy neighbor.>
    <i: Turn the other cheek.>
</list>
```

That was how we were told to be. That was how everyone had to be, from East to West, after the Maelstrom.

```
<list:item>
    <i: freedom>
    <i: charity>
    <i: equality>
</list>
```

This was the society Miach hated. Parents couldn't choose their children, but children didn't get to choose anything. "I would have at least liked to pick the world I have to live in," Miach

used to say. When the other boys and girls at school approached
her, she refused them politely at first. If they kept pushing, she
would say something like "I'm not interested in mere humans,"
and that would usually settle things.

She was like Princess Kaguya turning away potential suitors on
the grounds that they weren't from the moon or couldn't pluck
a jewel from a dragon's neck. This flat-out refusal to associate
with anyone worked like a charm. She didn't leave even the
starry-eyed would-be fans any room for interpretation. Of course,
if she really meant what she said, that would mean that Cian
and I weren't "mere humans." It occurred to me that maybe I
should have been upset about that.

The upshot was that I never felt like I fit in at school and
tried to spend most of my time holed up at home, though I did
somehow get dragged into one group or another during my years
there. I like to think of that as my last vestige of societal behavior.
I tried to hide in plain sight, praying that no one would call on
me to do anything in our extracurricular activities, thoroughly
weary of the kindness of friends.

```
<declaration>
    <Kindness always expects compensation in kind.>
</declaration>
```

The thoughtfulness of my teachers, of my parents, of everyone
around me was like silent suffocation. I'd heard once about
something they used to call *bullying*.

I wasn't really sure what it was like, nor had I learned much
about it then, at the young age of fifteen, but somewhere I had
picked up the vague impression that it involved kids acting in
a group to attack a designated target, usually another kid. This
had happened all the time at one point, but after the Maelstrom,
no attack on so valuable a natural resource as children would
have been permitted, not even if the assailants themselves were
children. Bullying had simply vanished.

Resource awareness.

That was how people defined their obligation to society. That and the concept of a communal body. Always be aware that you are an irreplaceable resource, they would tell us. "Life is the most important thing of all" and "The weight of a life is the weight of the world" went the slogans.

Had I been born a century earlier, would I have been bullied?

Probably, I thought. I wanted to be bullied. And I knew for sure that I wouldn't be the one doing the bullying.

≡

So I found her there on my way home from school, sitting in the park next to that jungle gym with something in her hands. It was only later that I learned what that thing was—dead-tree media, a book. Up until that point, I had been as largely ignorant of the past as every other high school student. I knew that parts of our history had been censored, images in particular, though I assumed they were of horribly disfigured corpses, or something like that. You needed special clearance to see those. The bulk of the visual media called movies couldn't be found on the Borgesnet because of the violence they depicted. Even what had probably been considered tame content by the standards of yesteryear was teeming with violence by the peaceful, elegant standards of admedistrative society. In order to see anything containing a visual portrayal of violence you needed legal credentials: an EVIL, or Emotionally-traumatic Visual Information License.

A license I have now because my work requires it, incidentally, but of course I didn't have one as a child. I didn't even know about them. Nor did I know about books, dead and gone a long time by then, nor had I heard that there was a pretty lucrative trade in them among enthusiasts. Girls in high school were so busy growing, where would one have even come by the motivation to learn about the past? Their heads? Their hearts? Their guts?

I wasn't annoyed by Miach's presence in the park that day. I merely acknowledged it, passing my gaze over her and moving on.

But Miach saw me.

Thrusting her book into her bag, she strode in my direction, taking big steps. I remember being surprised by her masklike expression. She had one finger thrust out, pointing at the jungle gym.

"You know why they synced the way the jungle gym moves to the children?"

I had no idea. Miach raised an eyebrow at my silence and went on. "It's so the kids won't die. Kids used to die on jungle gyms a long time ago. You know that?"

I shook my head. I was dumb. Both in the sense of being speechless and in the sense of being an idiot. I'd never heard of a kid dying by accident or even getting hurt on the jungle gym before. Miach talked like she was playing a flute, an entrancing tone that was as soft as it was cold and utterly devoid of emotion.

"At the beginning of the twenty-first century, jungle gyms were made out of metal—geometric lattices made of crisscrossing pipes."

"Kids would fall off the top?"

"They sure would. Jungle gyms back then didn't catch them like the ones do now. Metal bars aren't intelligent. They can't change, and they aren't even soft. Some kids hit their heads on the bars and died of skull fractures. And the sandboxes were breeding pools for viruses and bacteria. The park was a very dangerous place."

I hadn't the faintest idea why this person, arguably the strangest girl in class, was giving me an archaeological lecture on the history of jungle gyms. At least by then I had regained enough presence of mind to play along.

"So," I ventured, "what we call parks nowadays are very different from what they used to be."

She shook her head. "Not really. The look of the park hasn't changed for a century. There are trees and things to play on. There were kids back then who sat on benches reading books like I was just now. What's different is that the sand in the sandbox and the jungle gym and the climbing ropes weren't intelligent. They didn't *care* what happened to the kids that played on them."

"Sorry, that thing you were looking at just now, that's a book?" I asked.

"That's right, Tuan Kirie. I was reading a book. I always carry one around with me. I usually read it during breaks in class."

Miach pulled her book out of her bag and showed it to me. The cover read *An Unremarkable Man*.

"Doesn't sound that interesting."

Miach laughed at that. "As I thought! I know I have a tendency to fade into the woodwork, but still, I'm amazed you haven't noticed me before—that girl always off on her own, always reading some strange *thing*. You don't pay much attention to your surroundings, do you?"

How *hadn't* I noticed her? Practically the only girl who didn't join in any of the class groups, reading some strange artifact during recess? I thought for a moment that maybe no one had noticed her but immediately dismissed that. With all the initial interest in making friends with Miach, the other kids must have seen her, wondered about her. I was the only one oblivious.

"It's because you don't want to pay attention to people. You don't want to try to be friends. That's who you want to be, isn't it? You run with the other girls in their little groups, and you go out to volunteer on the weekends, but the person you're most concerned with is yourself. You don't give a rat's ass about harmony. That's why you didn't even bother to notice me and my book."

She was right.

She was right, and I was sure no one else but she had ever noticed this about me. It took me a while to regain my footing as I considered how to respond. All I managed was a completely tangential, and ultimately stupid, observation.

"Aren't books kind of heavy and hard to carry around?"

"Yes, they are heavy and hard to carry around, Miss Kirie.

Being heavy and hard to carry around is downright antisocial behavior these days, don't you think?" she said in a voice like a boy soprano's. And then she began to walk, holding her bag in her hands behind her back. I'm not sure to this day why I followed her. I only remember that it seemed as if what she said, her every word, was cutting into the heart of something I'd been unable to express for so long, and hearing her say it felt good. Or maybe it was that she had found an old blade inside me, rusty from seawater, and given it a bit of a sharpening. Incidentally, when I asked Cian about how she met Miach sometime later, she said she'd met her in the park too.

"So," Miach said, without turning around. "Q: if a person goes their whole life without falling from anything, how will they know what it means to fall?" I could only see the back of her head, but I was sure she was smiling.

"You're talking about the jungle gym."

"Not only that, but good enough."

"Isn't it instinct to be afraid of falling?"

It seemed to me pretty unlikely that someone could really go their entire lives without ever falling once, but even if someone managed it, I felt that somehow they would still have a fear of falling in their head.

Miach sighed, a sort of noncommittal sigh neither affirming nor denying my theory.

"So that's your answer? It's human nature to be afraid of falling—we're just made that way?"

"Yeah."

"Have you ever fallen off something?"

In fact, I had. It was when I was still pretty young. We'd gone camping, and I slipped off a boulder and fell into a stream. I could remember the instant it happened. You hear people talk about how time slows down during an accident, but for me it seemed like as soon as I realized my feet were slipping I was on my knees in the water.

I had scraped my leg on my way down, and when I looked at

it, I saw a thin line of color emerging from my right calf, curling off into the slightly cloudy water like a red ribbon. A little trout had gone swimming through it, and I thought he might get tangled in the thread, but of course he didn't. A moment later my father was helping me out of the stream. He used his portable med kit to fix my scrape, but I still remember what it looked like, that red thread of blood, drifting almost sensually in the water. The medicule paste—the same stuff that Miach claimed could kill fifty thousand people—quickly sealed the cut while the same medcare tank made antibodies to kill any infectious bacteria I might have picked up. My father attached the unit to the medcare port beneath my shoulder blade.

"What did it feel like, the moment you fell?"

Miach stopped and turned toward me. I answered honestly that it had been over so quick I didn't remember *feeling* anything. One moment I was on the boulder, the next I was in the water.

"Oh."

Miach shrugged and began walking again. I followed along behind.

"So you think someone who's never taken a fall in their life wouldn't be afraid of falling?"

"I didn't say that. But they could forget their fear. Just like we're forgetting what disease means."

"Disease is when you get older more quickly and your muscles stiffen up."

Miach looked over her shoulder, a smile on her lips. "That's what it means now, true, but that refers to only one condition that affects a few unlucky people with some unlucky genes. I didn't mean that kind of disease. I mean just getting *sick*. Like catching a cold or having a headache. Ever heard of those?"

I shook my head.

"In the past, there were lots of diseases in us, thousands. Everyone got sick, and this is only half a century ago I'm talking about. When the nuclear warheads fell during the Maelstrom, everyone got cancer from the radiation. The whole world was one big disease."

"Oh, I learned about that."

```
<reference:textbook:id=hsj56093-4n7mn 2jp:line=3496>
     <content>
```

Many people developed cancer from the radiation. At the same time, the radiation caused
mutations in China and the depths of Africa,
spawning a flood of unknown viruses. With
such a clear and present threat to its health, the
world transformed overnight from a capitalist
society monitored by governmental units to a
medical welfare society organized by admedistrative bodies.

```
     </content>
</reference>
```

"Right? I'm not sure why I have that memorized. Impressed?"

"Yes, but they never tell you about how people used to get sick
before then. You may have your history lesson memorized, but
you don't even know what a cold is. How could you? You've never
experienced one. Our society's accomplished a pretty amazing
thing. Thanks to WatchMe and medcare, we've driven almost
every disease off the face of the planet."

I hadn't told anyone at school who my father was—if they
knew anything, it was that he was someone important. Nuada
Kirie had been the first scientist to put forth the theory that
led to the technologies in WatchMe in a thesis he wrote with
an associate thirty-five years ago now.

```
<reference:thesis:id=stid749-60d-r2yrui6ronl>
     <title>
```

"Concerning the Possibility of Homeostatic
Health Monitoring with Medical Particle
(Medicule) Swarms and Plasticized

Pharmalogical Particles (Medibase)."

```
</title>
<author>Nuada Kirie, researcher</author>
<author>Keita Saeki, coresearcher</author>
</reference>
```

Did Miach know? What kind of face would she make if I told her? Would she hate me if I told her that this world she hated so much had all started with my dad? I wondered if I'd get a pardon if I told her that I too hated the world.

"You know we're living in the future," Miach said, her grim frown at odds with what should have been a positive statement. "And the future is, in a word, boring. 'The future is just going to be a vast, conforming suburb of the soul.' A man named Ballard said that. He was a science fiction writer. And he was talking about here, this place, *our* world. Our world where the admedistration takes care of everyone's lives and health. We're trapped in someone's antique vision of the future, and it sucks."

We walked on awhile until we came to a crossroads where Miach stopped and took me by the hand. I froze. This was different. She lifted my hand up before her face, with all the obeisance of a courtier before the queen, and said, "We've taken the mechanics of nature—things we didn't even understand before—and outsourced them. Getting sick, living, who knows what's next? Maybe even thinking. These things used to belong just to us, they could *only* belong to us, and now they're part of the market system, handled externally. I don't want to be a part of the world. My body is my own. I want to live my own life. Not sitting around like some sheep waiting to be strangled by some stranger's kindness."

And then she kissed the back of my hand.

I tried to yank my hand away, but I was already too late. The feel of her lips was permanently inscribed on my skin.

Cold.

That was my first thought. Her lips were cold. But it didn't feel bad; in fact it left a pleasant chill on my skin, like an aftertaste, that seeped down in between the cells. When I looked up, Miach was already across the street, heading in the direction away from my house.

"You and I are cut from the same cloth, Tuan Kirie," she called out, smiling again. Then Miach broke into a run and kept running until I could see her no longer.

≡

That was how I met Miach Mihie.

I walked by a park. She was reading a book. That was all.

It was enough to start a friendship that, short-lived though it was, would change the rest of my life.

03

Before I talk about my separation from and reunion with Miach Mihie, a story which begins in the Sahara, I should start by telling you about Cian Reikado's death by her own hand. It had been thirteen years since the three of us met. Forty-eight hours before Cian did a face-plant in a plate of *insalata di caprese* with

```
<list:item>
    <i:bright red slices of tomato>
    <i:pure white discs of mozzarella cheese>
</list>
```

and died, I was in the Sahara, in a world of painted blue and vivid yellow divided along a single line.

```
<landscape>
    <i: Blue sky as far as the eye can see.>
```

```
    <i: Yellow flowers as far as the eye can see.>
</landscape>
```

The colors met at the horizon, lush, permeated with pigment, enough to make anyone forget that the Sahara used to be a desert.

Forgotten by man, forgotten from history.

The shimmering waves of heat, the layered petals, even the gentle swaying of stalks in the breeze were all traces left by the painter's brush—a landscape turned into century-old art. A Mark Rothko abstract in yellow and blue. I sat looking out at it through half-lidded eyes from my vantage point atop a WHO armored transport. My lips relished the texture of the cigar they held, membranes of skin caressing the slight roughness of hard banana leaves. I enjoyed my illicit vice. Our caravan sat at the end of a vast sea of sunflowers, here in the place they once called the Sahara desert. Here, where the RRWs once fell.

```
<dictionary>
    <item>RRW</item>
<definition>
```

The Reliable Replacement Warhead, a type of warhead produced en masse by a nation called the United States of America, starting on or around the year 2010. These warheads were hailed as the "nuclear warhead of the twenty-first century," intended to replace the aging twentieth century arsenal with better durability, safety, and ease of use. During the Maelstrom which broke out in the English-speaking countries of North America in 2019, many of these warheads found their way to the Third World. And though EU forces, primarily those of France and Germany, intervened and were successful in disabling many nuclear sites, a final toll of thirty-five RRWs were lost from the American arsenal. Of these, fourteen were later recovered, two were detonated on American soil, and the remaining

nineteen were used in various conflicts around the world. (Excerpt from an International Atomic Energy Agency report.)
```
</definition>
</dictionary>
```

Thus the sunflowers.

It was an old method, yet still very effective. Whenever a war faded into peace, people planted flowers. The only thing different this time had been the scale of the effort. Enough yellow flowers to send a hippie crying for a flashback. It was old-fashioned phytoremediation. Genetically modified sunflowers sent roots deep into the soil, sucking up strontium and uranium and other pollutants along with the nutrients they needed to grow. In the course of a flower's life cycle, the land was cleansed.

As with so many other nations, the assembled countries of North Africa that so gleefully purchased nukes from unscrupulous characters in America during the Maelstrom and then dropped them with wild abandon here in their own land were now no more than a chapter in the history books. A brief scene in history's play from an age in which every war of independence bore the label "terrorism."

"They're here, *ma reine*."

Étienne called up to me from where he leaned against the side of the transport. He was wearing the standard pink medical troop–issue fatigues. Our guests would be coming, bearing gas lighters and cigars. I spotted a cluster of heads wrapped in blue peeking out from the admedistrative society–planted sea of sunflowers. They stuck out against the brilliant yellow of everything around them. The Kel Tamasheq had always worn those indigo turbans and veils, and they probably always would. They even wore them when they rode to war on camelback, which was impressive considering what terrible camouflage indigo made in a field of flowers.

Four Tamasheq warriors emerged from the lapping edge of the

sunflower sea, each with the traditional AK-47 on his shoulder. I got down from the roof of the transport and walked up to their leader.

"Greetings, woman of the medicine people. It has been some time."

"Greetings, warrior of the Tuareg."

The man in indigo shook his head. "Do you know what this word *Tuareg* means in Arabic?"

"Sorry."

"It means 'the people abandoned by Allah.' It is the name given to us by outsiders."

"So what does *Kel Tamasheq* mean then?"

"The ones who speak Tamasheq."

I couldn't help but think that "the people abandoned by Allah" sounded a hell of a lot cooler, and I told him so. Our gods, Asklepios and Hippocrates, watched closely over us, the "medicine people," and in their name we built temples to clinical medicine and struck down nearly every disease ever known to man. Our faith was such that we would continue striking them down, and so the medicine people would never be abandoned by their gods. We had even put WatchMe inside our bodies, just to make sure there was no place where the eyes of our gods could not see.

"You seem to dislike your own gods, woman of the medicine people."

"Yet you have no compunction about receiving their bounty from us." I had meant it as sarcasm, but the Tuareg smiled, white teeth against tan skin. "Yes, but the difference between us is that we worship only the minimum amount, no more. Luckily for us, the gods are very understanding about this arrangement."

I shook my head and sighed at the pragmatic wisdom of these desert—well, ex-desert—dwellers, and pulled a memorycel from my pocket.

"You think we bow too deeply to our gods, then?"

"In a word, yes. 'All things in moderation' you say, but you do not practice it. You are so filled with your faith that you must push it upon us as well. And this is why we fight."

"You don't think we represent the Nigerians, do you? We're not even an old-style government. We are an organization under the Geneva Convention, a consensus of medical conclaves—admedistrations—from all over the world. We're not allies of Niger, or the Tuareg for that matter. We're just an armistice monitoring group and not even a sanctioned branch of that."

"Whether you are Nigerian or of the medicine people it is all the same to the Kel Tamasheq. The only thing different is the surface—your skin. And sometimes not even that."

"Yes, but admedistrations are governmental systems. It's politics, not faith."

"Faith, imperialism—these are two words for the same thing. Niger may invoke this lifeism when they tell us to connect to their server, but it is just imperialism, plain and simple. In the past, we fought against the colonialism of England and France. When Qaddafi saw our bravery, he promised us glory as warriors, but the moment things went south, as they say, we were driven from his lands. We have fought dictators in Mali, Niger, and Algeria. All of them use the same imperialist hardware. Your lifeism is just new software for the same old machinery."

I sighed again. As a Helix agent operating as part of WHO, political negotiations were a large part of my work, and yet I found politics boring in the extreme. I shook the memorycel in my right hand.

"Then this med patch is imperialist software too."

"Which is why we partake only in moderation."

The warrior snapped his fingers, and the men behind him went back into the sunflowers. When they emerged, they were carrying several wooden crates between them. I knew what the crates contained—precious goods still enjoyed widely outside of admedistrative society and strictly forbidden within it. Things like the cigar I was still smoking, and booze, and a whole variety of other unhealthy delights.

"Actually, I'm a fan of moderation myself. That goes for Étienne over there as well, and for a great deal of people back at camp eagerly awaiting our return."

"Yours is a curious race. If so many of you desire to live in moderation, then why do you accept such rigid restrictions on your own person?"

"No, no, we moderates are in the minority. People like rigid rules and prohibitions, you know. They make them for themselves and live in fear that if they don't uphold the restrictions then things will go back to the way they were—the dark ages, chaos. That's basically it. For people living in fear, moderation just doesn't cut it. And most of the people in my world *are* fearful. It's like keeping a piggy bank when you never empty your wallet in the first place."

"What is this 'piggy bank'? A wallet, I've heard of."

"Actually, I'm not sure myself. About either of them. They're both from back when money was something you could put in your pocket."

Ancient words. The only reason I knew them was because Miach Mihie knew them.

"If your people could only learn the value of moderation, then there would be no war here."

"I'm sure you're right."

While the warrior and I spoke, Étienne and his crew received the crates from the Tuareg and began examining their contents. Étienne was French. While he was a bit too macho for my tastes, he had a discerning eye for beauty in his blood, and in my experience there were no people better at finding fault with things than the French. Nestled among the wood chips inside the crates was enough contraband to send any law-abiding member of admedistrative society into a swoon. Not that there would be any lack of those willing to partake back at camp. The moment these crates hit the ground, their contents would be divvied up. That was how it always was. Of course, we only opened the crates to the mob after Étienne's crew, our coconspirator who

downloaded the contents of the memorycel in my hand from
the admedistration server, and I took our cuts.

This was how I, as an adult, chose to give the finger to society.

The society that strangled you with kindness.

The society that knocked you out with a stealthy sucker punch
to the soul.

All you needed to break free was:

```
<list:item>
    <i: Pretend to accept adulthood.>
    <i: Trick the system into believing you were
    an adult.>
</list>
```

Just those two things.

They say that long ago, students who wanted to behave badly
had to sneak off to the lavatory or go behind the school gym in
order to smoke cigarettes. Another thing I learned from Miach.
What Miach didn't know was that the lavatory didn't cut it if
you wanted to smoke a fag these days. Now you had to go all
the way to the battlefield. Whether you wanted to see it as the
act of a lost soul or as the act of an idiot risking their life for a
little nicotine buzz, that was up to you.

I will state for the record, however, that before I got to this
place I tried a lot of different things, and I lost something very
important to me.

What I tried was overeating and self-starvation.

What I lost was Miach Mihie.

≡

Life.

The swarms of medicules my father and his friend unleashed
on the world drove the vast majority of diseases off the face of
the planet. The homeostatic internal monitoring system known

as WatchMe monitored immune consistency and blood cells down to the level of RNA transcription errors. What didn't fit was immediately removed. The little pharmaceutical factory found in every household, the medcare unit, instantly formulated the necessary cocktail of medicules for eliminating any disease-causing substances found in blood proteins. In a matter of milliseconds, the unit could pinpoint the area where it was needed most and send in the troops.

"Hey, Tuan, want to die with me?" Miach asked in her usual grand style. I looked around the room. Several of our classmates were still there, well within earshot. Miach was leaning over her chair, elbows on my desk.

Yes, it was a shocking thing for a high school girl to say, but to tell the truth, I wasn't surprised. I'd had the feeling it was something she was going to ask me someday. It didn't even surprise me that she chose such a public forum in which to ask. Nor would it surprise me if she had asked us to go right then. It had been clear for some time that suicide was our only way out of this place. We all agreed. Cian was standing right next to Miach, looking serious, waiting for my answer.

Now, I should explain that dying was no simple matter in those days. With the population so dramatically reduced, our bodies were considered public property, valuable resources to society, and as such they were something to be protected, or so went the publicly correct thinking.

In one of her many lectures, which she always delivered with that same nonchalant air, Miach had told us about how, a long time ago, the Catholics had been experts on the taboo against suicide. "You see, your life comes from God. You're given it by God, whether you want it or not. That's why mere humans weren't allowed to throw that life away, like a shepherd doesn't want his sheep offing themselves. People who committed suicide were reviled. They would bury them in the middle of an intersection so that they would never know the way up to heaven, not until Judgment Day. That was their punishment for betraying God's trust."

"I have a hard time imagining us being buried in an intersection," Cian said with an innocent smile.

Every time Cian smiled it made me inwardly groan a little. Miach ignored her and went on.

"And the successor to that Catholic dogma? Believe it or not, it's us, with our all-benevolent health-obsessed society. Bodies once received from God are, under the rules of a lifeist admedistrative society, public property. God doesn't own us anymore, everyone does. Never before in history has 'the importance of life' been such a loaded term."

Miach was right, of course.

And that was why we had to die.

Because our lives were being made too important.

Because everyone was too concerned about everyone else.

Of course, it wasn't enough to simply die. We had to die in a way that made a mockery of the health regime we were supposed to uphold by law. At least, that was what we thought back then.

"A long time ago, there were kings. When people wanted to change something, they killed the king. Usually, the killing was done by everyone, but not everyone could govern because the flow of information wasn't so good in those days. That's why they made governments. Then, if you got angry enough, you could kill your government instead."

The tone of Miach's voice seemed to ring clearer as she told us this, more finely honed than usual. It had a beauty to it, enough to send shivers down my spine. It was like a blade—a blade of ice.

"But what do we do now? In a post-governmental admedistrative society, there is no one to kill. Everyone is happy, everyone governs—the basic units of governance are way too small to target."

Miach looked out the window toward the front gates where our classmates were now stepping out into the street, on their way back home. From the third floor of the school building, you could look down on everything.

"Admedistration. The medical conclaves. A gathering of people who have reached a consensus on a particular medical system. The Harmonics. While an admedistration might have councilors, they're nothing like members of parliament used to be in the old governments. The councilors and commissioners just don't have the concentrated power of the old kings. We've divided power over such a wide area that we are effectively powerless. Even if we wanted to fight the admedistration like the students of old, there's no good government building for us to throw our Molotov cocktails at."

Cian frowned at that, a sudden unease coming over her. "So that's why we have to commit suicide? That's our attack on the system?"

Miach nodded firmly. "Exactly. Because we are important to them. Our future potential is their industrial capital. *We're* the infrastructure. That's why we'll take our bodies, their wealth, away from them. That's how we'll tell them our bodies are our own. We're no different from those who came before us; we're still trying to fuck the system. It just happens to be the case that the best way to hurt them is to hurt ourselves."

That was how Miach answered Cian's worries.

Of course, I'd be doing you a disservice if I didn't admit right here that most of the time how Cian and I felt was entirely subordinate to Miach's charismatic personality. We basked in her glow, hoarding it for ourselves.

Knowing so much, and hating so much, she was an ideologue. You always knew where she stood, which made her very easy to follow.

I don't imagine, even now, that I made my choice back then out of free will. I just had faith in Miach, who was always so clever, so well prepared. I knew she'd have the perfect way to strike back at the system. So when she brought her hand out in a clenched fist from her pocket and opened her fingers slowly, we knew with a cold clarity that it held our doom.

"See this pill? You only need to take one a day and it'll

completely shut down your digestive tract from your stomach all the way to your large intestine. One of these and your body will completely refuse any and all nutrition."

"Where did you get it?"

I had no misgivings whatsoever about taking the pill. I asked out of sheer curiosity as to the route by which she had obtained it. For a moment I imagined that she had, against all odds, managed to find one of those morally depraved adults—that anachronistic, extinct breed—living somewhere, and he had rented her body, and as luck would have it, he was a shady pharma dealer.

"I made it. With a medcare unit," Miach said, dashing my hopes. I knew she wasn't lying, either. Why would she? Cian came up behind her, putting her hands on Miach's shoulders, literally backing her up.

"Of course she did," Cian said. "Miach knows how to use medcare to make poison strong enough to kill an entire city. Making some pills was easy compared to that."

Without looking around, Miach reached up and gently laid one of her fingers on Cian's left hand.

In a lot of ways Cian was Miach's shadow. Like me, she felt uncomfortable in our world, like she didn't belong, but at the same time Cian was basically a coward who would do anything you said if you said it loud enough. She lived her life in fear.

Miach cleared her throat. "Well, I don't know about you two, but I'm dying." She looked at each of us in turn. "Cian? Tuan? What'll it be?"

I stared at the white pill in Miach's outstretched hand.

This little white jewel would cut my body off from every bit of nutrition it needed. I could eat my breakfast, lunch, and dinner with everyone watching, while that tiny forbidden fruit led me unerringly down the path of starvation. If we had been adults, the WatchMe inside us would send an emergency malnutrition alert to a health consultant's server, where it would yell and shout until the admedistration sent a fleet of ambulances to save us from ourselves.

So we had to do it before we became adults. In other words, right now.

Now was our chance. Now that we had met this genius, our savior, Miach Mihie.

If I passed up this opportunity, it would never come again, not for my whole life.

"I'll do it."

I don't know how long I stood there looking at the pill before I answered. Cian looked a little reluctant herself, but she nodded too. The classroom was already empty except for us three. Taking the pills in our hands, we tossed them in our mouths and swallowed.

Of course, I didn't die.

Thirteen years later, I was standing in the Sahara, blowing thick smoke from between pursed lips, waiting for Étienne and his gang to finish loading the crates into the rear compartment of our armored transport. The Tuareg—Kel Tamasheq—warrior was smoking one of the same cigars as the kind they had brought us. He was watching his men as they squatted on the ground a short distance away, opening a portable parabolic antenna.

"I've been meaning to ask for a while now, but what's with the dish?"

I had seen them bring it every time they came to trade with us. It was an antique communication device, the kind that you needed to use mechanical headphones with to hear. An unusual sight for a member of modern society, who was used to listening to her playlist of tunes on an embedded jawbone receiver.

"Huh? That? It is for sending ultra shortwave transmissions."

"Who listens to shortwave radio these days?"

"No one. Which is why we use it to communicate with our ally on the International Space Station."

That was a surprise. I had assumed that the ISS—a relic of the now-defunct United States of America—had been scrapped when its founding nation broke apart in the Maelstrom.

"Really? I had no idea anyone was still up there."

"Several of your admedistrations joined together to purchase it for the purpose of cultivating astronauts, you see. They're using it as part of a program to train particularly gifted students. One of our youths managed to beat out ten thousand other applicants—" the Tamasheq warrior slipped back his sleeve, an actor striking a pose, revealing a vintage wristwatch on his arm— "and he is passing over our heads at this very moment."

"I'm surprised they even let him in with his background, coming from a warring state and all."

"He grew up in Mali. He is a citizen of the Republic of Mali. We have many allies who are citizens of many countries. It is one of our strengths as a nomadic people."

"But what does he tell you from space? 'I have seen the Earth, and she is blue, like our turbans'?"

The moment I said it, the young man squatting by the dish with the bulky-looking headphones held up his hand. His face had gone pale.

The warrior glared at him. "Calm yourself. What have you heard?"

"We are getting a transmission...a bogey, a surveillance WarBird he thinks, flying toward our position. Probably Nigerian. But the silhouette is strange for a surveillance bird. He says they might be armed."

Étienne and his gang tensed. If their armistice monitoring group was caught on video trading with the Kel Tamasheq—even if they were only trading immunization patches for tobacco and alcohol—it would look very bad.

I sighed. "Now I see why you always went to such lengths to specify the place and time of our little meetings."

They were setting the times to coincide precisely with the orbit of that museum of a space station carrying their young spy inside. While we were monitoring the Tuareg, they were watching us too.

"Yes, without the support of our friend above, we would not be able to make these trades. This is a battlefield, you know. He is our spy satellite."

The Kel Tamasheq warrior thrust out his hand, and I placed the memorycel in it. People with WatchMe installed could use their own skin as a storage medium, transferring data merely by touching fingers for a few seconds, but the Tamasheq had demanded we bring the data inside this little rectangular crystal. Only then would they make the trade. They still only trusted things you could see with your eyes here. It was a kind of animism. Something physical had to be exchanged for there to be barter, and that was it. Even when the medium was essentially for show.

"This should work against the new infection that's been spreading in the area. Just install it on your server and your WatchMe will block off the access routes that the disease's prions are using."

I should pause at this point to mention, somewhat belatedly, that the Kel Tamasheq people all had WatchMe installed too. Sorry if I gave you the wrong impression or conjured some romantic image of a primitive, pure people, unsullied by medical nanotech. The Tamasheq weren't Mennonites or Amish. If something was good, they took it—in moderation. They were wise that way. If all it took was a brief injection, then sure, they'd install WatchMe in themselves.

So,

```
<question>
     <Q: Say you're the Tuareg, and you've all
     injected yourselves with WatchMe and created
     an internal health monitoring network. So
     you've been monitoring your peoples' health
     for a while, and you find this disease. What
     do you, as the Tuareg, do now?>
     <A: You can't do anything. No war-torn
```

```
      minority tribe has the money in their coffers
      to pay for an immunization program, even if
      they already have the distribution network
      in place. And the Kel Tamasheq medical server
      isn't attached to the admedistration network
      either. It's purely a local area network—an
      ethnic-area network, even.>
</question>
```

We had protected their server for them on several occasions. And now, we helped them by copying immunization program patches from our base server and trading them to them in secret.

In other words, our little illicit trade was saving lives.

All with programs filched from the admedistration.

```
<list:item>
     <i: We save lives.>
     <i: We get smokes.>
</list>
```

"The deal is made."

"And we're out of time." I gathered my long hair into a ponytail. "We'll be heading back to our 'temple' now, before Niger finds us here."

The Kel Tamasheq gave a hearty laugh. "If you hate your gods so, why not come live with us, woman of the medicine people? We treat our women with much respect. Especially now when there is war, women are very precious to us."

"Thanks for the proposal, but I'll pass."

"For what reason?"

"For the very reason that I'm here in the first place—because I'm a coward."

For three or four seconds, the Kel Tamasheq warrior looked at me in silence. To show that he understood and was sorry on my behalf.

I could talk the talk, but I was thoroughly unable to leave my admedistration, to escape the society into which I'd been born. No matter how much I wanted to leave. And why was this? In a word, fear. No matter how much I hated it, I couldn't bear to see it all go away.

It was this fear that:

```
<list:item>
    <i: Left Miach to die alone.>
    <i: Left Cian and me to remain.>
</list>
```

I think I just wasn't strong enough to follow Miach to the other side.

I wasn't brave enough.

That was all the Kel Tamasheq warrior needed to hear in order to understand. His wrinkled, dark face, burnt darker by ultraviolet radiation, broke into a broad smile—a father's smile. He stuck out his hand for a shake.

"Then we will meet at our next exchange, woman of the medicine people. If you should change your mind and wish to join us, you are always welcome."

"At the next exchange, then, warrior of the people who speak Tamasheq."

It was enough for me to know I had a place where I could escape.

The kindness the Tamasheq warrior had shown me was of a completely different variety from the forced charity I had grown up with. It was the sort of kindness that grew only in the harshest environments, among a people who had fought hard for their freedom against a long line of imperialists and dictators.

Both I and the warrior turned away then and walked back toward our own people.

"A little faster, *ma reine*!" Étienne called from the passenger seat window of the transport. I waved at him to quiet him down and went around to the other side, hopped in the driver's seat, and gripped the wheel.

04

```
<declaration>
    <i: My job is to start wars.>
    <i: At least everyone seems to think so.>
</declaration>
```

It wasn't always like this. Things had been different, albeit some time before I entered the agency.

The Helix Inspection Agency was part of WHO, the World Health Organization.

In the beginning we were like the International Atomic Energy Agency, but for genetics rather than nukes. It was our job to visit any admedistration facility doing research on genetic engineering to make sure nothing was being produced that could potentially be a threat to humankind. We were supposed to monitor the technology, that was all. That was around when the "helix" got attached to our name.

However it happened, the scope of our operations expanded wildly over the years until we were basically a flag-waving troop of diplomats-cum-peacekeepers charged with the protection of life everywhere—not to put too fine a point on it. As Miach used to say, no one who waves a big flag is up to any good. So we would wander into other admedistrations and even some old-style governments to check whether they were ensuring their populace a lifestyle that was sufficiently "healthy and human"—a recipe for conflict if there ever was one. We were like a hand grenade loaded with the seeds of mass mayhem, one our elders had gleefully passed on to us for reasons I couldn't begin to fathom.

This was the place I had chosen to be my escape from the world.

As nations gradually downsized their functions, leaving only a smattering of military and police forces, stewardship of the planet's economy fell to the massive number of admedistrations that rose in their place. Unlike the now-obsolete national governments, admedistrations were smaller units, operating on shared principles of medicine, thoughtfulness, and charity—which meant if they saw a neighbor suffering, they couldn't just stand back and leave them to their own devices. Even though Niger was ostensibly still an old-style nation, the reason for their altercation with the Tuareg was none other than a misguided attempt to force the Kel Tamasheq to link to the Nigerian medical server—"To ensure the nomads a more healthy lifestyle," they said.

The Kel Tamasheq's response, of course, was "Fuck off."

The sociologists expressed the guiding principle behind the Helix Inspection Agency and ostensibly, the Nigerian government, like this:

```
<dictionary>
        <item>Lifeism</item>
<definition>
```
A politically enacted policy or tendency to view the preservation of health to be an admedistration's highest responsibility. Based on the welfare societies of the twenty-first century. In practical terms, this means the inclusion of every adult in a homeostatic health-monitoring network, the establishment of a high-volume medical consumer system with affordable medicine and medical procedures, and the provision of proper nutrition and lifestyle advice designed to mitigate predicted lifestyle-related illnesses. These activities are seen as the basic minimum conditions for human dignity.
```
</definition>
</dictionary>
```

We Helix agents were the elite soldiers of lifeism. That was how many people saw us, at any rate. And it was true enough that, when we did mobilize after receiving requests from several admedistrations, what I would write in my subsequent reports would oftentimes lead the parties involved directly to war.

With our current Sahara situation, the agency hadn't even decided which side we were on. As I said before, the Tuareg had installed WatchMe, and they were using that fact to argue that they were not the anti-lifeists the Nigerians said they were.

As the self-appointed judges of all life, the Helix Inspection Agency never wanted for critics with axes to grind—sometimes quite literally.

```
<list:item>
    <i: shooting>
    <i: stabbing>
    <i: strangling>
    <i: poisoning>
    <i: bombing>
</list>
```

These were just some of the varied ways in which no fewer than twelve Helix agents had died in the line of duty. This was the job I had found for myself, traipsing to every war zone in the world, inviting hatred at every turn—a senior inspector at the tender age of twenty-eight. Due to the dangers inherent in the job, I had trained in how to use most modern weapons and more than a few primitive ones as well.

Which was why it made sense for Étienne—whose machismo was undercut by an utter lack of combat experience—to call to me for help from the gunner seat of our armored transport.

```
<shout>
```
   "We have a problem, *ma reine*! They're going to see us!"
```
</shout>
```

"Oh, they've probably already taken several pictures," I muttered to myself, then shouted over the whine of the transport's engine and the creaking of the suspension, "You think it's a standalone?"

"Probably," Étienne shouted back. "Niger knows the Tuareg use electronic countermeasures, so there's a good chance the WarBird flies silent."

"Someone's highly trained, hopped-up bald eagle then."

"The brain, yes. But the body is a soft composite. Plenty of hard points on the wings."

"A surveillance bird packing heat? That's a bit odd."

"This *is* supposed to be a no man's land. If anyone's out here, it would be either the Nigerians themselves or the Tuareg. Why wouldn't they come armed?"

"Well, as long as they really are on their own and don't get any images of us back to their HQ, we're fine."

I told one of Étienne's men to drive for me and gave him the wheel. Moving into the back compartment, I pulled out a lethal-looking cylindrical object stashed next to the crates of cigars and booze—something the Kel Tamasheq warrior had thrown in as a "bonus."

"Get down from the gunner's seat, Étienne. I'll handle this."

"What do you mean *handle*—"

When the Frenchman looked down from his perch and saw what I was holding, every muscle in his body froze, causing his hands to slip from the railing. Étienne fell past me down into the passenger compartment. Not that I blamed him. It wasn't every day you saw a girl cradling a more-than-a-century-old RPG launcher under her arm.

"Tell your man driving to keep us going straight. Whatever he does, I don't want him jerking the wheel one way or the other."

"Got it," came the muffled reply. Shamelessly violent launcher in hand, I stuck my torso out through the rooftop hatch.

"You sure you can handle that thing, Miss Kirie?" I heard Étienne's voice from the floor of the transport below.

"Better than you can," I replied quietly, then gave the trigger a squeeze.

For all their sophistication, WarBirds were fairly artless things when it came to flying. They never zigzagged or circled, just flew straight toward their target like this one was flying toward us right now. All I had to do was fire my gift from the Kel Tamasheq into the air directly behind us to ensure a fatally explosive midair rendezvous.

```
<list:item>
     <i: wings covered with hard points>
     <i: a body and fuselage controlling the wings>
     <i: a living animal brain fused with a neural net>
     <i: a little bit of armor plating>
</list>
```

What had been the bird scattered in the sky in a brief flare of plasma—a daub of bright paint haphazardly added to the blue and yellow landscape.

"Combat glasses!" I shouted, thrusting my hand down into the compartment without taking my eyes off the sky behind us. Étienne passed up his binoculars and I quickly scanned the area. No more WarBirds in sight.

"Nothing at a low altitude, at least. Let's keep an eye out though," I announced as I ducked back inside the transport.

I let the now-empty launching tube roll on the floor, and I collapsed, feeling the tension drain from my limbs. After I had caught my breath, I undid my ponytail. Free from its restraint, my hair swirled, brushing across my forehead and cheeks.

Smoking cigars was tough these days. Getting your hands on them in the first place was even harder. My mind, newly released from the vice-grip of tension, was whimpering inside my skull, wanting to see nothing, hear nothing. *Why not? Étienne can get us back to the base. I'll just sit here quietly until we're through that security gate.*

I closed my eyes and let a soft sleepiness come over me. Waves of fatigue, lapping at my temples.

≡

The swift realization came the moment I opened my eyes. *I failed.*

The light on the ceiling glowed with a soft, pale pink light.

I was lying on my side, surrounded by machinery. There were tubes attached to me—not just the one on the medport below my collarbone, but attached the old way too, with needles. I was in an emergency room at a hospital. Or maybe an emergency morality center. It only took me a little while to realize which it probably was.

I was alive. Which meant I had failed.

Not just once, but twice.

This hadn't been the first time I'd attempted to kill myself with food. A while before I'd even met Miach Mihie, I'd been carried to a center just like this one after overeating. I don't think I had consciously decided to die that first time. It was more of a vaguely defined longing toward death that had been rattling around inside my skull for years before I finally decided to take action.

```
<disappointment>
```
Overeating didn't kill me. Neither did undereating.
```
</disappointment>
```

"Not again," I mumbled, even though by then I had realized that my mom was sitting right there next to my bed.

This is it, this is the time I die. I had been so sure of it. How foolishly optimistic I had been. All I needed was Miach and the tools—the weapons—she gave me, I'd thought, and I'd make it for sure. If she could make a device capable of mass murder out of a household medcare unit, she could do anything.

If I couldn't do this thing even with her help, then I'd live my entire life without being able to do it at all.

How completely dependent on her I was.

"You're awake," my mother said, then she began to cry. It was like what I'd said hadn't even fazed her. Or maybe my throat had been too parched for her to make out the words. Who cared, anyway? I was the one that would have to live with my failure, not her.

"What about Miach?"

This time I was sure she heard me. I saw her frown a little, her eyebrows drawing together. I asked her again.

Somewhere over my head, a children's bio-monitor was softly chirping away.

I wouldn't need one of those if I were an adult. They wouldn't need any external devices to tell what was going on inside me. Not with WatchMe installed. Not with a swarm of medicules tattling on everything going on beneath my skin at all times.

"Miach . . . didn't make it," my mother said, chewing her lip. Like it was her fault.

I wanted to vomit.

```
<anger>
    Don't do that, Mom.
</anger>
```

My mouth remained closed, but inside my thin, motionless body, I shouted: *Don't do that! Don't feel guilty about someone else's death! She had nothing to do with you!* It was this world— the one that demanded you sympathize with everyone, even people you'd never met—that I couldn't stand. The air reeked of kindness, with the awareness that everyone was public property. The only acceptable form of thought was a public correctness that compelled you to blame yourself for not being able to stop someone from committing suicide—even if there was no conceivable way you could have.

But I lacked the stamina and the will to shout it out loud, so I simply muttered, "So she died."

My mother nodded, dabbing at her eyes with a handkerchief. "Cian's okay, though. She's being treated at a different center."

"Oh."

The pharmaceutical regime and counseling that came next dragged me, kicking and screaming, back into society's fold.

```
<list:item>
    <i: Out of the world of hypokalemia.>
    <i: Out of the world of hypothyroidism.>
    <i: Out of the world of osteoporosis.>
</list>
```

Back to the world of constant, mandated health.

With daily counseling and daily pills, I dug the ditch of my failure ever deeper. At least I had the common sense not to let my counselor know how I felt about it.

It came to me as I was riding home from the center in a taxi with my mother.

I was sitting next to her, looking out the window at the evening sun on the Sumida River. The calm serenity of the buildings lining both banks chilled me to the bone. They were all painted in pastels—pink, blue, green—all of them just a little off-white.

There weren't any laws against painting a building something more exciting, and yet here they were, an endless line of houses, all cast in bland, nondescript shades. None of them stood out against the others. Nothing to disturb the eye, and therefore nothing to disturb the heart.

```
<hopelessness>
    There's nothing I can do.
</hopelessness>
```

It was then that I learned how to give up. Miach was dead, and she had accomplished nothing. I lost all hope in the world and, at the same time, learned how to live without hope.

I looked out the window and saw the evening sun on the twelfth of June, 2060, shining down on a giant hospital ward stretching to the horizon on both sides of the river. Mankind was trapped in an endless hospital.

```
<regret>
    I'm sorry, Miach.
</regret>
```

I couldn't do it. And it had taken the sacrifice of a life to the gods of medicine for me to understand. I started to cry there in the backseat of a taxi. My mother's eyes remained fixed forward on the road ahead, as though she didn't notice. After I cried myself out, I leaned back in my seat and fell asleep.

≡

I opened my eyes again.

Tuan Kirie, senior inspector, age twenty-eight.

Étienne was shaking me by the shoulder where I lay next to the crates of cigars and wine.

"We are at the base, *ma reine*."

05

The "blushing maiden brigade."

That was what people called the medical corps. I think they meant it as a compliment.

If you were wondering whether every admedistration's medical corps wore pink uniforms, you were right. Go to France, Russia, or Mexico, and every medical corps uniform, helmet, and armor transport was painted the color of a lightly ripened peach. Like the army always wore drab olive, and the navy black and white.

Which was why the tents in the Niger armistice monitoring camp were all pink.

Against the sea of pale pink, the deep crimson coats we Helix agents wore stood out. We stood out everywhere, for that matter. Now I was making my way through the tents, back to where the crates were being unloaded—our backyard.

I carried off the portion for myself and for our server techie—call him Alpha—and left Étienne and his crew to handle the rest of it. I would get back to my own office as quickly as possible and drink myself into a stupor, as I always did. At least, that was the plan.

I had zero interest in knowing the details of how Étienne divvied up the booty from the Kel Tamasheq, or how much money he made, or how much he skimmed for himself. He would always pass me some credit after we were done, so I knew he at least wasn't stealing everything. That was good enough for now. All I needed were smokes and booze. That was it.

```
<list:item>
    <i: Things to damage my lungs.>
    <i: Things to damage my liver.>
</list>
```

In my world, you had to come all the way out to this hinterland, to a battlefield, just to find ways to damage yourself. Effective, yet ultimately trivial ways. Far more trivial than what I had attempted back in high school, before I lost Miach.

"I brought the goods," I announced, stepping past the pink flap of the tent where Alpha worked—where I found not only Alpha surrounded by his infield terminal screens, but also my boss with an excessively stern look on her face. I caught the look of abject fear on Alpha's face and realized things had taken a decided turn for the worse. "We were waiting for you, Senior

Inspector Kirie," the woman in the crimson coat just like mine announced.

"You needed to talk to me about something, Os Cara?"

"Only about what that is you're hiding behind your back."

I shrugged and tossed the vintage wine in her direction. I had a reputation for giving up easily.

She caught the ancient Petrus, the ruby red liquid sloshing inside the glass bottle.

```
<dictionary>
    <item>Château Petrus</item>
<definition>
```

Brand name of an alcoholic beverage originating in France's Pomerol region. A "bordeaux wine." Noted for its label depicting Saint Peter, the twelfth apostle. This château wine vaulted from relative obscurity to immense popularity after winning a gold medal at the 1889 Paris Exposition. One of the most expensive wines in its heyday, after the Maelstrom and the ascendance of lifeism it shared the same fate as all other alcoholic beverages.

```
</definition>
</dictionary>
```

It had already been over forty years since anyone in a developed country had been able to freely enjoy alcohol. "What do we have here?" Os Cara breathed as she caught the bottle of forbidden pleasure lightly in her left hand. "I would ask if you have no shame, but then, I already know the answer."

"It's called wine." I snorted. "Heard of it?"

She didn't even look at the label. "A bordeaux. Lots of merlot in these—100 percent in some barrels, depending on the year. Makes for a very smooth texture."

"No shit."

"Most certainly not. I drank one of these when I was much

younger, actually. The last generation that could truly relish alcohol. We had a Petrus just like this one in my house."

"I hear it was quite expensive," I said, stepping closer to the trembling Alpha and my boss, even as I felt like I was walking into a trap.

"My family was quite well-to-do before the Maelstrom."

"You don't say," I said, now standing directly in front of my boss. Prime Inspector Os Cara Stauffenberg.

```
<notes> Anointed the cherub of Helix agents; at
Geneva HQ she's known simply as 'Prime.' Single.
Age seventy-two, with the looks of a beautiful
woman in her late thirties due to ultrahigh reso-
lution WatchMe, a perfect control system, regular
antioxidant treatments, and periodic removal of
accumulated RNA transcription errors. </notes>
```

"Well, this won't do." She presented the bottle. "You know how embarrassing something like this is for us."

"I haven't lost all capacity for rational thought, if that's what you're suggesting, Prime," I said, my smile thin.

She glared at me. Alpha, sweating bullets, shrank back into the shadow of his monitors. He wasn't even seeing us there anymore. His eyes were looking off into the distance somewhere, probably at the wreckage of his career.

"At least you seem to be aware of your own wrongdoing. However, you clearly do not comprehend where we are and what we're doing here."

I had to laugh at that. It was precisely *because* I knew so thoroughly what kind of place the Sahara was that I had specifi-cally requested a transfer here. There was silence again until my boss spoke.

"The Nigerian armistice monitoring group is in an extremely delicate situation at present. The report that we Helix agents submit will determine which of the two parties, the Nigerians or the Tuareg, had the right of this conflict."

I shrugged. I was pretty sure that if it became known we were partaking of smokes and booze, the Tuareg would probably consider us their allies, what with their predilection for living a life of moderation. This was apparently not the scenario my boss had in mind, however. She began to walk around me in a tight circle.

"The monitoring we do on behalf of admedistrative society must not be allowed to itself incite more conflict. If word got out that we, who by all rights should be the upholders of lifeism and champions of long life and health, were indulging in such harmful substances as alcohol and tobacco, it would be a disaster."

A disaster for whom, I wondered. It certainly wouldn't bother me any. I wasn't harming anyone with my secondhand smoke. And shouldn't I be allowed to harm myself as much as I pleased? *No*, I immediately corrected myself. Even *thinking* that was verboten in this age of public correctness.

"What I want to know is how you kept your own WatchMe silent all this time. Any amount of alcohol consumption should trigger the medicules in your system, which would immediately inform the health supervision server—"

"Well, being out here in the sticks and all, the server does go off-line pretty frequently," I said, as though my boss really needed an explanation of conditions here at the armistice monitoring camp. "And besides, we girls know a little magic. That is, those of us who still remember that we're girls."

"That's very funny," she said without a trace of humor in her voice. "I don't know what underhanded means you used to get this contraband, but I will have you know what damage your actions have caused to our operations."

"I already know: none."

I clapped a hand on her shoulder as lightly as I could. In her crimson coat, Os Cara Stauffenberg quaked with rage. I ran my finger gently over the embossed snakes curling around the staff of knowledge on the WHO badge she wore. "I wouldn't worry about your badge getting tarnished, Os Cara. Because you're not going to tell anyone about this, are you."

Os Cara clucked her tongue. It occurred to me that this was probably the most dramatic expression of disdain she, a dyed-in-the-wool member of admedistrative society, could muster.

```
<anger>
```
"Of *course* I can't go public with this."
```
</anger>
```

She glared at me. "If the authority of this agency were to be impugned, then all our efforts to make this world a healthier, more peaceful, more charitable place will have been wasted. Even in the short term, were I to go on the record about your little 'party time,' our monitoring operation here in Niger would lose any and all credibility overnight."

```
<sarcasm>
```
"So sorry to hear that, Prime."
```
</sarcasm>
```

At this point, Alpha seemed to realize that things might not be as terribly bad as he'd imagined them to be. I gave him a pat on the shoulder as well, saying, "I certainly hope nothing of the sort happens to our wonderful operation here."

```
<yell>
```
"I'm not finished!"
```
</yell>
```

Alpha resumed his former state of rigid terror.

"I'm afraid you're going to have to take responsibility for what you've done, Senior Inspector Kirie. You will be returning home on the next available flight and remain until you've seen the error of your ways."

"Home? You don't mean Japan…"

No fucking way.

After all I'd done to escape that gulag—the overeating, the starvation, the loss of a friend—all ending in the pursuit of my current career flying from one war zone to another.

No fucking way.

"That's right. Japan. I won't have you using this battlefield for your recreation room. You betrayed us. I want you to go back and experience what it's like to truly love and be loved by your neighbor, Tuan. You *will* learn how to be publicly correct."

My boss set the bottle of wine down by one of Alpha's terminals and strode out of the tent, leaving me rooted to the spot. I was already beginning to imagine the days of depression ahead of me. I would be living in Japan. The place I hated as a youth, the place Miach detested with all her heart. Japan.

"You're incredible," Alpha whispered, a sigh of relief escaping his lips. "Simply amazing. I can't believe you got off with such a light punishment. I'd heard you were a powerhouse, Tuan, but that was something else. No wonder Étienne calls you his queen."

I felt the sudden urge to slap the cheerfully babbling Alpha hard across the cheek, but instead of allowing myself to resort to violence, I picked up the wine and slammed the entire bottle of Château Petrus in one breath. A stream of the ruby liquid spilled from the side of my mouth and ran down my chin, splattering over my crimson Helix agent's coat. Alpha swallowed, his momentary elation evaporating more quickly than the wine on my collar.

I needed this. I needed to be able to drink like this. It might be my last drink in a long time.

My heart sank.

Sayonara, Sahara.

Catch you around, Kel Tamasheq.

06

And so I found myself stranded in the desert called normal life. A vast wasteland of public correctness and people as resources. Stuck in a sinkhole called harmony.

I could see it spreading out from the airport like an oily film on the land. Forming a gestalt that made me want to retch. I spotted clusters of residential buildings below, square little blocks in inoffensive pastels. Like tiny multiplying pixels of artificial life on a monitor. The PassengerBird I was on flexed its wings, tracing a soft circle through the air. An announcement sounded near my inner ear, telling me to prepare for landing.

An RPG comes flying out of nowhere, slamming into the side of the PassengerBird.

The giant bird flies into pieces, raining down its contents—the passengers—on the little Cubist residents far below. In death, the bird looks just like the WarBird I shot down over the Sahara. The men in suits spill out of its body cavity so lightly and evenly, just like in Golconde <notes> Rene Magritte painting, c. 1953 </notes>. *On the ground, the residents waste no time flinging off their pretenses of charitable love to pick up baseball bats with which to knock the falling men back up into the air.*

As the bird touched down on the runway I realized I had been daydreaming. The other passengers were already standing from their seats, getting ready to disembark. I grabbed my bag, left the bird, went through luggage screening, and spilled out with the rest of the bird droppings into a burgundy-colored airport lobby.

The moment that I stepped off the PassengerBird, the augmented reality in my contacts kicked in. Just about everything in my field of vision had AR metadata associated with it. I glanced at the entrance to a café and saw the menu hanging in midair with a meter next to it telling me how many seats were empty and next to that some stars indicating favorable reviews.

Everything in our world had a user review attached to it.

Even people had little social assessment stars stuck on them.
Café de Paris in the airport lounge: four stars.
Tuan Kirie: four stars.
Cian Reikado: three.

```
<shout>
    "Tuan! Tuantuantuan!"
</shout>
```

A little girl's voice shouting my name.

Since I didn't know any little girls, I was pretty sure it had to be Cian Reikado. She was one of the only people who knew I was coming back. I went to pick up my Helix agent code at the baggage counter, then turned to Cian, who was yelping and jumping with excitement. If she'd had a tail, she'd have been wagging it for sure. Some public metadata was attached to her body—the name of the admedistration she belonged to and the `<notes: social assessment> SA </notes>` score she'd been assigned by her admedistration's moral consortium.

"How'd you find me in that crowd?" I asked.

"What are you talking about, Tuan? You stand out in any crowd!"

"Oh?"

"You should really watch that—you probably attract enough attention as it is with your job and all. Wow, you're really, uh, rough-looking too. No offense."

"Comes with the territory. I can't help it if battlefields always tend to be the deserts and the highlands and the swamps. It's tough on the skin."

To tell the truth, my skin condition probably had more to do with my various indulgences than any battlefield conditions. The only thing keeping my WatchMe from alerting the nearest admedistration-contracted counselor was the DummyMe I'd installed to send phony data about my body to the server, but the DummyMe fell short when it came to fooling the human eye. I must've stuck out like a sore thumb.

```
<list:item>
    <i: a daily pill from the medcare unit>
    <i: an appropriate lifestyle chart from your
    life designer>
    <i: health food designed to leave a minimal
    footprint on your body>
    <i: appropriate health counseling>
    <i: a medicule swarm to eliminate the blemishes
    on my skin before they turn malignant>
</list>
```

Having bad skin meant you weren't living up to at least one of the basic requirements of lifeist society. A sure sign you were a wrench in harmony's cogs. Lifeist society meant everyone, man or woman, had to conform to certain standards. Nonconformity made itself physically obvious.

Bad skin? A sure sign of poor self-control.

Shadows under your eyes? A lack of proper publicly correct resource awareness.

All of this was reflected in your SA score. The vast majority of admedistrations required all adults to make their histories, including their medical records, public knowledge. This was, in part, to make the process of assigning a social assessment score as transparent as possible. No doubt, if politicians these days were as fat as the leaders of old had been, such open sharing of personal information would never have come to pass.

I remembered my surprise when I came across pictures of great leaders while leafing through historical archives.

There they were, unadulterated, men and women of power, and most of them were grossly overweight.

Judged by modern standards, someone like Churchill could never be considered a hero. Who would trust a man as copiously fat as that? Any nude painted before the eighteenth century was completely out as well.

I came across an old schoolyard rhyme once.

Fatty fatty, two-by-four, can't fit through the bathroom door!

```
<question>
      <Q: What does the word fatty, repeated here,
      mean?>
      <A: It is a pejorative term referring to a person
      who is overweight.>
</question>
```

Words like "fatty" hadn't been used in years—too great a risk of hurting someone's feelings. Not that there was anyone chubby enough to rate the term anyway. Like alcohol, tobacco, and the morally depraved man who paid money for sex with girls, these terms of belittlement had simply faded away. They were soon followed in their extinction by fat people and even skinny people. All gone. Under the constant monitoring of WatchMe and the constant advice of a health consultant, obesity and emaciation both had been driven out of the human experience.

I looked at Cian, my friend who had tried to starve herself to death along with me and Miach.

Her body fit perfectly within the prescribed margins for a healthy adult.

A boring body, in a boring adult size.

I quickened my pace across the airport lobby—itself designed with incredible attention paid to reducing any feeling of oppressive authority the structure might have naturally possessed. A cluster of yellow tables stood out against the burgundy interior, grabbing the eye. As I headed for the subway, dragging my bags behind me, Cian made an effort to match my pace. It was incredible really. For all the vast space here, and the high ceilings, I couldn't detect a whiff of authority to the place. Admedistrative design was sterile like that. By their very nature, large architectural spaces had a certain fascist scent to them, a prideful authority that came from being monumental and leaked out whether the builders intended it to be there or not. Large structures made human beings small by comparison. Even public places, like this airport, did that.

Which was why the designers of the place had pulled out all the technological stops to reduce the impact of the airport's size. I could sense the attempt to cover the unwanted stench of power, and it made me sick to my stomach. Calling the place a monastery made it sound too Christian, but it was true that the world we lived in often felt like it was being run by nuns. It was fascism, courtesy of Mary, Mother of God.

The world had been made thoroughly gentle. Even the arts.

My profiling sheet—just one of a multitude of health-maintenance applications I had to use in my daily life—was like another version of me.

A version of me that accepted everything the real me hated.

My profiling sheet lived inside the admedistration server from where it monitored my daily routine, identifying my likes and dislikes and keeping a careful eye out for anything, be it literature or an image, that might cause me emotional trauma. Any novel or essay I was about to read would be scanned in advance and cross-referenced with my therapy records. If any content therein touched on a past trauma I had experienced, it would often be filtered out before I ever saw it. At the very least, I would receive a warning. *This work of art contains potentially emotionally damaging material*, or my favorite, *This novel contains possible violations to the general morality code, article 40896-A as determined by the Health and Clarity Admedistration Moral Review Board of 4/12/2049.*

When all possibility of fear was removed from our environment, a more subtle kind of fear replaced it.

<recollection>

"Do you know something?" I heard Miach say. "A long, really long time ago, there was this artist who used an airplane and smoke to write the word *BANG* in the sky over Hiroshima. What do you think?"

"*Bang*, like the atomic bomb? That's in pretty bad taste, I'd say."

"It's totally in bad taste!" Miach said, grinning. "The artist got so much criticism that he had to publicly apologize. Because his art made some people unhappy, it hurt people's feelings. But no one would even *do* that kind of thing these days. They'd be warned away from it by the admedistration before they even got to it. They probably wouldn't even have the idea in the first place. With these filters warning us what we're about to see all the time, no one looks at anything. How could an artist get any bad ideas to start with? I look at old books and paintings and I envy the imaginations of our predecessors. I really do."

"Why?"

"Because there was always the chance that they would hurt with their art. Always the chance they would make someone sad or angry."

</recollection>

My eyes fell on an old man, a custodial worker, cleaning the airport. Clearly, he hadn't been paying as much attention to his health as he should have. His SA score was about as low as it got. A low SA score brought job security of a kind—no one would dream of taking your job away from you, out of pity—but it also meant an utter lack of mobility. You were basically stuck doing whatever it was they made you do. That said, the old man was very likely leading a fairly comfortable life, thanks to food distributed by volunteers and a living support center where he could sleep at night. He might've even had some family.

Cian was slightly shorter than I was, so when we walked side by side, she had to lengthen her strides just to keep up. When I walked, I didn't care whether I was matching anyone else's pace or not. I had decided that was how I was going to walk a long time ago. Right after I'd lost Miach.

And there it was. Walking together with Cian brought on the

feeling of loss I had dreaded was out there somewhere waiting for me. Miach should've been standing right there, right by Cian, book held behind her back, telling us in great detail (without actually looking at us) how we could damage the world in which we lived.

It was like Cian and I were a temple from which someone had stolen our golden Buddha named Miach Mihie. I couldn't help feeling like there was this space in front of us that should have been filled.

Odd that being together with someone should remind me of what was missing. Our charismatic leader, gone these thirteen years. She carried far too much knowledge in her tiny body, and far too much hatred, and far too much beauty. And now she was gone.

```
<recollection>
```
I want to dance on the graves of those kind, healthy people.

A waltz, I think.
```
</recollection>
```

A nonexistent Miach looked back at us over her shoulder. Miach Mihie. Miach Mihie. Miach Mihie.

We passed by volunteers handing out artificial protein soup to political refugees in the airport lobby and took the elevator down to the floor where the subways connected to the airport. On my way down, I had the sudden sensation that Miach was standing right behind me, and I had to turn and look, but it was only Cian.

"You going home?" she asked me as we waited on the subway platform. The platform had been painted an inoffensive sea blue.

I shook my head. "I'll look for a hotel or find someplace to crash. There's nothing for me at home."

"I wouldn't say that. Everyone wants to hear your stories,

you know."

"Who's everyone?" I chuckled and shook my head. "Actually, I did get a message from one of the neighbors saying they wanted to throw a welcome home party. They were going to call everyone for two blocks around and be here waiting when my PassengerBird landed. Can you imagine? No thanks. That's the last thing I need. Especially since my mom was so enthusiastic about the idea."

"Why not let them have their party? It could be fun."

"I have nothing to talk to them about."

"What are you saying? You could tell them about the Sahara, or where you were before that—Colombia, was it? You've been to so many places and seen so many things, Tuan."

Yeah, I could tell them stories. Like the one about the child soldiers drugged up and made to shoot their own parents and siblings for target practice. Or the bloody severed arms and legs piled up in heaps like firewood. Hardly anyone who bought into the admedistration's protected life had the faintest clue about the realities of war. They were far too busy being nice to everyone in their immediate vicinity to care. Cian was as ignorant as any of them. Ignorant and innocent. Nothing had changed in that regard.

"And I think they'd want to hear about what you've been doing," Cian was saying.

"I'm just not interested." I sighed for effect. "Cian, you volunteering at all?"

"A little. Three days a week. Delivering meals and taking care of the elderly, that sort of thing."

"Morality sessions and health conferences?"

"Online, yeah. About fifteen hours a month. It's not too bad."

What was this? One of my friends, a girl who couldn't stand this world, who tried to kill herself just to leave a mark on its perfect face, had conformed completely to a typical, publicly correct lifestyle.

Or maybe it was less personal. Maybe it was just that kids grew up and became adults.

```
<definition>
     <i: To become an adult is to:>
          <d: Install WatchMe.>
          <d: Accept the dictates of an
          admedistration.>
          <d: Attach oneself to the admedistration
          server.>
          <d: Receive lifestyle directives from some
          health consultant.>
          <d: Show up for conclave sessions, both
          online and off-line.>
</definition>
```

Miach's ghost hovered nearby, a cold smile on her lips as she whispered.

This body, these tits, this ass, this uterus. These are mine. Aren't they?

So after our failure, Cian had taken the plunge headfirst into the adult world. The only one dragging her heels was me, and I couldn't decide whether that was admirable or pitiable.

I hung, suspended in space, somewhere between Miach Mihie's ghost and Cian Reikado's innocence.

"Look, Cian, I've been overseas a long time, right? So I just don't know the people who live around my home. I haven't volunteered with them or gone to health meetings with them. I'm just not very connected to the community."

I explained to her that being a globe-trotting Helix agent meant:

```
<list:item>
     <i: dangerous working conditions>
     <i: difficulty fitting in with social life in
     any one place>
     <i: difficulty forming bonds with former
     neighbors or a medical community>
```

```
<i: an artificially high social assessment
score given to make up for all that>
</list>
```

Because we lacked a conclave to assess us, the admedistration awarded us an arbitrary SA score in order to account for the inconsistency that resulted from doing something very important to the continuation of the admedistration's lifestyle while, by necessity, being forced to operate independently of that admedistration.

"Oh. Really?"

"Really."

As I was explaining my life to Cian, I couldn't help but feeling that I had somehow become Miach. Miach explaining how to use a medcare unit to make a chemical weapon capable of killing fifty thousand people. Miach who could make a pill that would shut down your entire digestive tract.

Miach who could wear a cool smile as she told you she wanted to watch the world burn.

I felt like she must have back then, filled with knowledge no one else had, talking openly, brazenly, full of confidence, fearing nothing, giving every word a declaration.

Hey, Cian, did you know that if you install DummyMe, you can spoof your physical data before it gets sent to the server? Hey, Cian, did you know that you can do anything to yourself with DummyMe installed? Hey, Cian, have you heard about this… Hey, Cian… Say, Cian…

But instead of playing Miach's doppelgänger, I merely smiled cynically and said, "The real reason they give me a score is because if they didn't, I'd be labeled a sociopath."

Cian frowned, not understanding. "So you're not going home?"

"Probably not."

Cian stepped in front of me. "Then let's go get something to eat, at least. There's this new building near where I live. It looks all bumpy and white from the outside, like it was made out of solid plaster. But when you go inside, you can see out. It's this new intelligent material, a special light-refracting Styrofoam glass."

"Sounds pleasant. I'm really not in the mood."

"We could eat, and then you can come over to my house. It's only eleven o'clock. How about lunch?"

I had an urge to check with the nonexistent Miach. *"Want to go with me and Cian to get some lunch?"*

I sighed and told her I'd go with her to lunch. Only lunch. I followed after Cian, getting into the first bean-shaped light yellow train that came sliding down the tracks. My WatchMe linked to my credit account, deducting the appropriate rail fee. I was just realizing how long it had been since I rode the subway in Japan when I looked around at the other passengers and felt a sudden fear grip me.

<panic>

They were all the same. Everyone.

It hadn't been so blatantly apparent on the battlefield. Working with an international group meant there were a lot of people from a lot of different places and races around all the time, and more than a few of them were indulging on the sly, like me.

That was definitely not the case here.

For the first time, I realized how bizarre a sight the medically standardized Japanese populace presented. The difference between the couple sitting in the seats nearest to me was no more than the difference between mannequin A and mannequin B. Neither was too fat nor too skinny. Every person on the train conformed to a particular body type. Everyone fit within a healthy target margin. I felt like a stranger in a house of mirrors—a country of mirrors.

How had things come to this? How could everyone be the same when simple genetics told us everyone was different?

<maxim>

The more rigid and narrower the goal, the easier it will

be for the weak to achieve.

</maxim>

Miach's phantom again, whispering in my ear. Talking just like she always did when giving us a lecture. I remembered her saying how human will could grow rigid even while it succumbed to temptation.

Humans were like a broken meter whose needle swung back and forth between desire and willpower, always all or nothing, never lingering in between. There was no room for moderation. Even a pigeon had a will of its own. Volition just happened to be a good fit for vertebrates, which was why our brains kept it around.

</panic>

"Is something wrong? Do you feel unwell? Here, take my seat," a woman offered, seeing the momentary fear caused by social panic flash across my face. My AR told me that she was a politician—a coordinator or commissioner for an admedistration somewhere—though her face looked no different from anyone else's. She too was well within the margins. A healthy, standardized face. It was a feature—that is, the lack of distinct features—I assumed you would find even more the higher up you got in the chain of command. I remembered everyone at Geneva headquarters looking more or less the same.

"I'm okay," I told the politician and went a short distance down the train car. Cian caught up to me, a worried look on her face.

"You shouldn't have walked away like that. It's rude. She's an admedistration councilor somewhere."

"I know. I saw the AR. Sorry."

"I think you're just exhausted from work, Tuan. It must be hard, doing all that. But you're really making a contribution to society."

Me, making a contribution to society.

Making a contribution by going to a battlefield where I could smoke.

Making a contribution by consciously choosing not to be part of society—where I undoubtedly would have either slashed my own wrists or cut into someone else a long time ago.

Which was how I was able to agree with Cian, without a trace of sarcasm, that I was indeed making a great contribution to society.

My path and Cian's had diverged sharply after Miach's death. For Cian, all the enmity she had felt toward society, her family, her hometown, and school had passed. For her it was like a rite of passage, a phase everyone went through before returning to a standardized life. For me, I had gone on collecting the knowledge I surely would have gotten from Miach were she still alive, and on the surface, I too appeared to be conforming, just like Cian. My grades kept climbing until I took Miach's former place at the head of the class. In a sense, I *had* become Miach's doppelgänger. I was becoming Miach Mihie.

Cian wasn't becoming Miach. She was joining a club—a club at least nine out of ten Japanese belonged to. A club with tightly defined body fat ratios and stable immune systems and known RNA transcription error rates.

All while I went from party zone to party zone. Battlefield to battlefield.

From airport to airport.

Cigar to cigar.

Bottle to bottle.

Except this time, I'd gone from Château Petrus to *insalata di caprese*, in a place where there was little likelihood of seeing a single smoke or drink.

I had said goodbye to the depressing, dizzying subway and now sat enjoying a healthy meal in an Italian restaurant with my old friend.

There were slices of tomato burying water buffalo cheese that had been completely drained of fat, with a light sprinkling of olive oil on top. We were on the sixty-second floor of the Lilac Hills building. The meals here were noteworthy for each bearing a slight risk to the diner.

When you ordered a plate, the menu displayed your total calorie intake and any potential risk of chromosomal damage you might suffer from consuming the food. Every single item on the menu had a warning attached. Once you had read the risk information to your satisfaction, you could order what you wanted to eat, within the prescribed limits set for you by the health consultant on contract with your admedistration.

There were a few other people in the restaurant, but not too many. Everyone sitting around the marigold tablecloths were just like the people I had seen in the subway, each well within the margins of a healthy Japanese body.

<sentiment>
> "It's been a long time since we ate together," Cian said, watching the server arrange our *insalata*. It occurred to me that since the day we had both tried to throw our lives away and failed, Cian and I hadn't eaten together once.
>
> "No kidding."
>
> "It's a little strange, actually, being here with just the two of us."
>
> I looked out the window at the view from the sixty-second floor.
>
> The view that Miach wanted to mar.
>
> The view that Cian had gotten used to.
>
> The view I had escaped from.

</sentiment>

"Actually, I think this might be the first time we've ever eaten together without Miach. Just the two of us, I mean."

"I think I ate alone with Miach a few times," I said, " before she brought you into things."

"Yes, I think you're right. You were friends before I met you, weren't you?"

"I wouldn't call us friends. We didn't find each other. Miach pretty much grabbed me."

"Really?"

"Yeah. I was walking along one day and she literally ran up and grabbed me. Remember the story about the jungle gym?"

"Oh, right."

"Wasn't it pretty much the same way with you, Cian? With me she asked me whether I knew why the jungle gym twisted and warped like it did."

"Maybe she was casting a net."

"Huh?"

"I mean, she was sitting in the park reading a book, right? Maybe she was waiting for someone to notice her? A girl like me or you."

Miach, waiting for someone to notice her? Something about it didn't fit with the image I had. Miach hated everything about healthy society. She hated how everyone worried about everyone else, offering help whether it was asked for or not. It didn't make sense for her to want out of the system and then go looking for friends. I told Cian I didn't agree.

"Huh? Why?"

"I just think you're wrong about her. Miach wasn't looking for friends, she was looking for kindred spirits—comrades in arms."

"Isn't that the same thing?"

"Not really. They're both kinds of acquaintances, in a loose sense of the term, but the bond between kindred spirits isn't friendship *per se*. It's more like the bond between fellow soldiers."

Picking up knife and fork, I cut off a bite-sized chunk from my *insalata*. Cian was looking at me, clearly trying to comprehend what I was saying and just as clearly failing.

"See, Miach didn't want friendship," I continued. "She wanted someone to fight by her side. You can't fight a war alone, you know."

"The more the merrier?"

"You bet. Of course, it'd be a lot easier if she could find someone who already shared a lot of the feelings she had about things. So you're right in that she was lying in wait for us, just for a slightly different reason."

"We weren't really the soldiers she hoped we would be, were we, then. At least, I wasn't."

Cian was probably right. Miach clearly identified the enemy and charged ahead all by herself. We were basically no better than deserters.

If Miach had been saved as we had been, would she be sitting here today, eating lunch with us? Would she have a smile for her former soldiers who fled the front lines? I had no idea.

It was then that I noticed Cian looking at her plate with a strangely expressionless face. It was bizarre. Like her plate was a pool, and she was watching something swim at the bottom. Her eyes remained fixed on one spot, unmoving. I was about to ask what was wrong when Cian opened her mouth, her eyes still fixed on her *caprese*.

"I'm sorry, Miach," she whispered, then suddenly, her table knife was in her hand. Before I had time to wonder what she was doing, Cian had thrust the tip of the knife into her own throat.

"Ehgu," said a strange voice from Cian's mouth.

```
<silence>
<surprise>
```
Summoning some strength I never would have imagined to be in her, she twisted the table knife inside her throat and brought it straight through her carotid artery and out one side. The knife couldn't have been that sharp. Her strength was unbelievable. It was as if her neck had been a tree trunk, and she had cut halfway through it with one blow of a hatchet.

Blood sprayed from her neck.

The blood splattered all over the interior of the Italian restaurant on the sixty-second floor of the Lilac Hills building, painting the walls in patches of somber red. A shower of blood caught the server—who had just been coming to our table to fill our water glasses—directly in the face. He passed out.

It all happened in a single, endless moment. All I could do was stare. Blood flowed down onto her plate, mingling, but not blending with, the olive oil dripping down from her salad.

```
</surprise>
</silence>
```

The other customers began to scream.

Just as, at that very moment, similar screams rose up across the globe.

Because, at that very same time, by a number of various means, 6,582 other people also tried to take their own lives.

```
</body>
<etml>
```

<part:number=02:title=A Warm Place/>

```
<?Emotion-in-Text Markup Language:version=1.2:enc
oding=EMO-590378?>
<!DOCTYPE etml PUBLIC :-//WENC//DTD ETML 1.2
transitional//EN>
//<etml=lang=jp>
<etml=lang=en>
<body>
```

01

```
<flashback:repeat>
      <re: I'm sorry, Miach.>
      <re: I'm sorry, Miach.>
      <re: I'm sorry, Miach.>
      <re: I'm sorry, Miach.>
      <re: I'm sorry, Miach.>
```

Cian, whispering in my memory.
Her last words on infinite repeat.

```
      <re: I'm sorry, Miach.>
</flashback>
```

"We've confirmed 2,796 deaths," the communications officer from Interpol explained. On the same day, at the same time, 6,582 people all attempted suicide, and a little less than half of them were successful.

I subtracted the number of successful suicides from the total number of attempts: 6,582 minus 2,796 equaled 3,786.

For 3,786 people, that fateful moment was less than fatal.

The communications officer in my AR projection was still talking. Apparently several of those involved who had survived their initial attempt eight hours ago were in critical condition, meaning the total death toll could still rise.

Those "involved."

Apparently, it had taken Interpol and all the senior Helix agents participating in this AR gathering quite some time to decide exactly *what* to call them. Were they victims? Suicides? For so many to attempt to end their own lives at the same time, they had to have been under some kind of influence or had been, indeed, victims of some sort of coercion. Yet look at any one of the people in the resulting pile of corpses and you had to think they did it themselves, all on their own.

```
<public_opinion>
     <i: Everyone agrees suicide is a selfish,
     shameless act.>
     <i: —A direct assault on the body, a public
     resource.>
     <i: —Stark evidence of an appalling lack of
     awareness of the public nature of one's own
     body.>
     <ex: As far as I'm concerned, if someone wants
     to off themselves, they're welcome to it.>
</public_opinion>
```

Okay, people were allowed to grieve, fine. If one of my friends died, I'd grieve. But to sit back and judge someone else's choice, someone completely unrelated to you—to talk about "public property" and "resource awareness" when someone just *died* to justify giving someone's life a cold look? That was what I called arrogance, and I wanted no part of it.

Miach would have thought the same thing. Rather, Miach *did* think that.

But not the rest of the world.

The only reason the suicides weren't punished was because they were dead.

Beyond the admedistration's reach. Finally.

If someone were to come up with a way to effectively punish the dead, I'm sure the world wouldn't hesitate. I knew the regimen of drugs and counseling awaiting the failed suicides—it would be an earnest attempt to reclaim the resources the "involved" very nearly squandered, to patch up these damaged goods and put them back on the assembly line. To reinstate them as the basic unit in the medical economy, so that they could fulfill their societal function as consumers. Cian and I knew how that went. Been there, done that.

Except Cian wouldn't be coming back this time.

Suicide was an offense punishable by disdain. Even if it wasn't technically a legal offense. I remembered Miach telling us how the Catholics buried their suicides in the middle of a crossroads as punishment for betraying God.

Admedistrative society, lifeist society, hadn't quite figured out how to treat suicides yet. The gravediggers wanted to know if they were victims or perpetrators. *So, uh, ma'am? Should we just go ahead and dig this hole in the crossroads here, just to be safe?*

People had no idea what to do. I didn't blame them. Lately, not even battlefields produced this many corpses. In lifeist society, it took old age, accidents, and the occasional, very rare homicide to result in a body. Otherwise, people just didn't die. Cancer and other diseases were targeted in real time by WatchMe and removed. The all-important credo that was resource awareness helped us keep ourselves in check. Keep your WatchMe updated and your body fat ratio low.

The people who had killed themselves eight hours before were suspended in space over a chasm that ran between criminality on one side and victimhood on the other.

I participated in the Interpol/Helix session from my hotel room. The Helix Inspection Agency had called the AR meeting after determining that this event was something in which they should be involved. Clearly, a crime had been perpetrated against the highest value of our society—the very sanctity of life! Even though no one was sure exactly what the crime was, there was a general expectation that they would figure that out shortly to everyone's satisfaction.

"Those involved," the Interpol communications officer told us, came from twenty-five different countries, and all belonged to the Sukunabikona Medical Conclave, or Sukunabikona Admedistration, as it was more commonly called. The means by which they had killed themselves were varied:

```
<list:item>
    <i: scissors>
    <i: chopsticks>
    <i: jumping off buildings>
    <i: hanging themselves>
    <i: cutting their wrists>
    <i: chain saw>
    <i: table knife>
</list>
```

And numerous other ways besides. It all made for a very impressive list of recipes for self-destruction.

The chain saw had been a guy in forest management. He had been in the middle of work and went from sawing through a tree to sawing off his own head. The one with the chopsticks had, in the middle of a meal, driven one chopstick through an eyeball and then twisted it around and around for good measure. It made sense that eating utensils took a prominent role in the list, since in every single confirmed case, the "involved" had simply picked up the nearest potentially lethal item they could find and gone for it.

```
<list:dialogue>
    <d: Say, I could probably push this pin
    through my carotid artery.>
    <d: My, this chain saw would be perfect for
    cutting off my head!>
    <d: Huh, you think if I drove the chopsticks
    through my eye I could reach my brain?>
    <d: Hmm, I daresay that rope is perfect for
    hanging oneself!>
</list>
```

As far as Cian's method went, she was strictly by the book.

"This *event* is clearly an act of terrorism against admedistrative society!" the Helix agent next to me was saying. He was a senior inspector assigned to monitor elections in some war-torn hinterland. Of course, I say "next to me" but that was merely where the AR conferencing system had placed him. In reality, I was sitting all alone on my hotel room bed, talking to people who weren't even there. If anyone had walked in and seen me they would have thought I had gone mad.

```
<boredom>
```
An act of terrorism. How perfect.

It was the kind of statement that sounded meaningful while being utterly pointless. You might even call it a waste of time, but in our lifeist society where harmony was valued above all else, no one smirked or shook their heads at my neighbor's blatant grab for attention. Instead, they all nodded and muttered their agreement that yes, that had been a most insightful statement. They had to.

That was how you did things as an adult.
```
</boredom>
```

Maybe it was because I had seen one of my old friends become "involved" right before my eyes that this whole meeting felt like a charade. I didn't have time to sit here listening to all these people blow smoke up each other's asses. I waited the minimum amount of time necessary to not seem rude, then asked what condition those involved were in now.

The Interpol agent turned toward me. "All those who did not immediately die have fallen into a deep comalike state. At present, not one is available for questioning as to motives."

"What about WatchMe?"

The question came from the Helix agent who had just been spouting off about terrorism. The Interpol agent turned, politely smiling at the man's ignorance. "Though it is not widely known, WatchMe does not monitor the brain's condition."

"Really?" the agent asked, looking at me for some reason.

"Yes," the Interpol agent said. "WatchMe cannot penetrate the blood-brain barrier. Apologies in advance if you already know this, but the blood-brain barrier is a feature in the body that limits the circulation of materials between tissue fluids—such as blood—and the brain. The barrier is there to protect the brain and spinal column from potentially dangerous substances, and no scientist has been able to develop a medicule able to pass through. Basically, it's a blind spot in the system."

"Doesn't the blood-brain barrier work like a filter? Why can't they just make a medicule smaller than the holes in the net?"

"Actually, the barrier is *not* like a net. Though in fact it was believed to be for quite some time. A century ago, the popular theory was that anything with a molecular mass of, oh, 500μ or less would be able to pass through, but that theory has since been entirely refuted. As it turns out, certain kinds of material, no matter what their size, cannot pass through the blood-brain barrier, while rather large molecules can pass through if they are needed by the brain. In other words, size doesn't matter. The blood-brain barrier isn't a mindless filter, it's a highly attenuated and complex selection organ."

The man looked down at his lap. "I see."

I smiled. This was about the closest thing to a smackdown I

was likely to see in one of these meetings.

"Though the numbers are small, there are a handful of instances every year of people with WatchMe installed dying of brain tumors and otherwise preventable hemorrhages. The brain is the last sanctum of the body, you might say. The only place where WatchMe's eyes cannot go. That is, most of the brain. Because the pituitary gland and pineal gland deal with hormones, we can access them.

"Of course, we are doing what we can to monitor the coma patients externally via electronic scanning, though that falls far short of nano-level resolution," the Interpol officer explained. "That said, only eight hours have passed since the…outbreak. We have, at present, no confirmation of any brain abnormalities in those affected, but it is still quite early in the day, so to speak."

I saw Prime Inspector Os Cara Stauffenberg stand. She was probably still in her pink tent in the Sahara. For a second, I felt like she might be glaring at me, but I was too busy ignoring her to see.

Would Cian have killed herself if Prime hadn't sent me packing from the Sahara? Would Cian really have stuck a knife into her own throat if I hadn't been sent back to Japan to go to lunch with her and watch her do it?

Or would she have done it anyway, with a knife she was using to cut tomatoes in her own kitchen?

```
<memory>
```
Want to fill a bathroom with poison gas? Beyond easy.
```
</memory>
```

Hadn't Miach said something like that?

```
<maxim>
```
Every person holds within themselves the potential to take another's life.
```
</maxim>
```

I've got the power.

I could kill someone.

Even myself.

Each of us holds within us the power to destroy something important.

Had Cian killed herself, after a thirteen-year delay, just to truly understand the meaning of Miach's words for herself? Was I to be the only one left behind?

"In two hours from now at a general emergency meeting of WHO in Geneva, I will be addressing all admedistrations and telling them that this, this chaos, is evidence of a full-on attack against lifeism," Prime announced.

"As senior inspectors, all of you will be cooperating with security in your local regions. You all know about the treaties binding each admedistration to WHO—we're going to make them honor those treaties. I want each of you to take the initiative in rooting out the people responsible for this, and let them know we will not sit idly by while they threaten our very way of life."

Every agent in the room nodded. Like that, the session ended, and I was back in my hotel room, surrounded by unpacked bags.

Unlike the other inspectors, I didn't have much time. I had to start right now.

<recollection>

Just two hours earlier, our fearless leader Prime Inspector Os Cara Stauffenberg had opened a secure session in AR with me.

<scorn>

"Though it is not public knowledge, you are under house arrest. Add to that the fact that you witnessed one of the people involved take her own life, and it is clear that you cannot be allowed to be involved in the upcoming investigation. Let us not forget that as a recent victim of an emotionally traumatic experience, you have likely sustained psychological damage. Most admedistration ordinances dictate that any conclave member who has experienced a dramatic ordeal must submit themselves to a minimum of one hundred twenty hours of psychiatric counseling and drug therapy. Your presence will not be required at the emergency meeting of Helix inspectors to be called in two hours time."

</scorn>

I laughed. Of course I should be involved with the investigation. And seeing my friend kill herself was emotional trauma? Really? If I'd suffered an emotional trauma, it was when I failed to die at the age of fifteen. No, it had been when I tried to kill myself by overeating, long before I met Miach Mihie. Don't talk to me about psychological damage. I've been damaged for years.

<laugh>

But I didn't say that. Instead I saluted Prime Inspector Stauffenberg and informed her that I would happily use my newfound free time to work on my press release informing the media just how many of us in the Niger armistice monitoring camp had collaborated in acts of shameless, wanton indulgence.

</laugh>

She had asked me if I was serious.

"Deadly serious."

<press release>
    <i: Confession, part I>
    <d: For over half a year, we copied immuniza-
    tion patches off an admedistration server
    without authorization and provided them to
    the Tuareg, who were involved in an armed
    conflict at the time.>
    <i: Confession, part II>
    <d: In return for providing this, we received

```
crates filled with shamefully harmful sub-
stances, such as alcohol, tobacco products,
and, once, even hallucinogens.>
<i: Confession, part III>
<d: We installed copies of DummyMe, available
on the black market, and used them to spoof
our physical data in order to deceive the
health consultant server.>
</press release>
```

I wanted everyone living in every admedistration across the world to know exactly what we did, even if that revelation should happen to take the fragile state of truce between the Nigerians and the Kel Tamasheq and throw it off a cliff, leading to the loss of countless lives and the complete gutting of the Helix Inspection Agency as it lost all authority in the aftermath.

Also, I added, if my memory serves, due to the nature of our work in conflict zones, Helix agents are given a five-day reprieve before they are required to report to mandatory therapy following a traumatic incident, ma'am.

I was satisfied to see a shiver run through Prime Inspector Os Cara Stauffenberg as the sheep's clothing came off her misguided, insubordinate underling. Clearly, she was wondering how someone with such a deeply flawed character could have sneaked her way into the upper ranks of an elite division of WHO.

Except I knew she wasn't trembling at me. She was trembling at the unseen, unnamed specter of Miach Mihie standing right behind me. At times like this, I often felt like it was Miach's words coming out of my mouth.

I counted roughly thirty seconds of rage, regret, and hesitation passing before Prime spoke again.

"Fine. You will participate in the investigation."

I nodded, satisfied.

"However," she added, "though you may have a reprieve, don't dream you're getting out of therapy. Not even *I* could do that. Five days from now, you will be placed in an emergency morality center to undergo a full therapeutic regimen."

This was about the worst that Prime Inspector Stauffenberg could threaten me with, and nothing she was saying was news. Unfortunately, she was right. The mandatory therapy requirement would be a very hard one to get out of. In five days' time they'd toss me in an emergency morality center somewhere, pile on the kindness and thoughtfulness until I couldn't breathe, and when I cried uncle they'd keep me in their benevolence-stained sweatshop a few weeks more just for good measure. As long as I was a member of an admedistration, there was no way around it.

I had five days. I only hoped that would be enough time to figure out why Cian had died.

</recollection>

02

<movie:ar:id=6aehko908724h3008k>

That day, Ichiro Tokume found the perfect rope in his storage closet.

The image was completely Ichiro's POV, so I couldn't actually see him, though I knew what his face looked like from a little data window in the lower right-hand corner of my field of vision.

Ichiro Tokume; life pattern designer; 38.

These were the people that designed how other people should live. It was a branch of health consulting.

They would look at your hormonal balance, blood sugar levels, CRP, GTP—the works, all supplied by WatchMe—then determine a lifestyle pattern to optimize both their client's health and their social assessment score. They would devise lifestyle "recipes" that told their clients what to eat for breakfast, lunch, and dinner; what sports they should participate in; and the most efficient place for them to go to volunteer in their free time.

Planning out someone's daily life.

Planning out someone's life.

It wouldn't surprise me if Ichiro Tokume himself were following a life design given him by some other health consultant. That was how you lived in our postconsumer society.

Now this life planner was deftly working his fingers, holding the rope up where he could see it, and tying a knot to make a loop. Somehow, I didn't think what he was doing had anything to do with his hormonal balance or GTP or any of that.

Next he walked into the kitchen where he found a small stool—probably something his wife stood on when she needed to reach the top cupboards. I watched him pick it up and return to the living room where he had been tying his rope. There he stood on the stool and began looping the other end of the rope around a light fixture in the middle of the ceiling.

Again his field of vision lowered as he stepped down and began to walk through the house toward the bathroom. (*I wonder what he's up to?*) I watched him turn on the water, then everything went dark as he closed his eyelids. (*He's washing his face.*) When he next opened his eyes, Ichiro Tokume was wiping his face with a towel. I caught a glimpse of his expression in the mirror for only a moment.

Not a trace of emotion.

Empty eyes, open mouth. Three empty holes.

Back to the living room. The noose was swaying gently from the ceiling. As he stepped up onto the stool he looked down at his feet, then back up. The noose encircled my field of vision and then was gone, around Ichiro Tokume's neck. My field of vision shook violently.

Now we were swaying back and forth, looking out at the living room interior. A soft-pink sofa. A screen on one wall. Intelligent wall material made to look like plaster. We turned a full circle around the pivot of the rope, as though Ichiro wanted me to see where he lived with his wife. Everything was recorded.

Come in, come see my home!

This is the living room. This is where I hang myself.

Of course, I was merely watching what his AR contact lenses had recorded. Ichiro Tokume, age thirty-eight, had expired when the full weight of his body had pulled at the vertebrae in his neck. If I'd wanted to, I could have watched the feed until his body stopped providing its electrical current to the lenses and it went dark—a nice natural stopping point to the record of his last few minutes on earth.

```
</movie>
```

First-person POV suicide flicks.

Of the 6,582 cases, 2,049 had been wearing AR contact lenses when they did the deed. The last things they saw remained on the server, giving us close-up front-row seats to their deaths.

AR contacts monitor focus points, and I wanted to see what Ichiro Tokume had been looking at. A cursor blipped around the screen, highlighting wherever his eyes went. The objects and angle of view were then listed up and run through several formulas to analyze Mr. Tokume's mental state in the ten minutes leading up to lights out. The results, displayed in bold on another screen, were nothing surprising.

Severe depressive tendencies.

Suicidal tendencies.

I decided to watch a hundred more similar movies at 3x speed. Each was about twelve minutes long. Divided by three times one hundred equaled four hundred minutes.

I plugged in the commands and sat back, for just under seven hours, to watch the deaths of one hundred people randomly selected from 2,049, back to back.

My database of suicide movies.

I couldn't imagine anything other than a mass, unexplained suicide requiring the creation of such a morbid collection.

Each person in the database had only ten minutes' worth of footage, the reason being that all had taken action so swiftly. It was like each of them had parents who had told them to never put off for tomorrow what could be done today, and they listened. The logger in Canada had been cutting through a particularly large pine tree when he suddenly pulled out the chain saw and cut through his own neck. I watched his field of vision lurch, then fall until it was rolling across a bed of matted decaying leaves.

The scene changed to the next victim.

```
<movie:ar:id=8dhkie470267k9948s>
```
I was looking at my own face, from another time and place. My breath stopped.

Mirror, mirror, on the wall.

She had been among a random selection of a hundred victims.

I was staring at me. A dead person was staring at me.

I looked at myself, Tuan Kirie, through the eyes of my friend who, in a matter of minutes, would stick a table knife through her own throat and paint the walls of the restaurant with her blood.
```
<silence>
<fear>
```
My face. Skin tanned a little by the ultraviolet rays of the Sahara.

What a grotesque mirror.

The Italian restaurant on the sixty-second floor of the Lilac Hills building.

The field of vision went from my face down to the bright

red and fresh white slices on her plate—the *insalata* we'd
both ordered. I noticed everything was moving at normal
speed and realized I must have flicked off the fast forward
without even realizing it. The cursor told me Cian was
focusing on the red slices of tomato and brilliant white
slices of mozzarella layered atop them.

```
<horror>
```
    "I'm sorry, Miach."
```
</horror>
```

    That was what Cian would be saying any second now.
    I heard the words moments after anticipating them.
    Cian's attention shifted to the table mats, and I saw
her healthy arm and hand, neither fat nor slim, slide into
view. The hand grabbed the knife to the right of her dish,
gripping the handle with the blade pointing down, while I
stared. A waiter walked up to fill my glass of water—

```
<limit:patience>
```
    I switched off the AR.
```
</limit>
</fear>
</silence>
</movie>
```

My lungs were screaming for air, my brain for oxygen. I had
forgotten to start breathing again.
    The sound of my heaving breaths filled the conference room of
the WHO Japan branch I was using for my little viewing session.
    Thankfully, I was alone in the room. I had been the only
Helix agent in Japan when the event occurred, which was lucky
for me. This way I wouldn't be obliged to cooperate with any
other agents.
    Maybe I *should* go in for immediate therapy. Maybe I should
go to some emergency morality center with white cotton walls
to escape from the words that had spilled from Cian's mouth.
    Calm down. Steady breaths.

Don't you want to find out why Cian died? Didn't you blackmail your boss just for a chance to find out what your friend's last words meant? So you saw yourself looking at your friend just before she died, so what? You're breathing heavy just because you remembered a few words?

I'm sorry, Miach.

And then something occurred to me.

Of my one hundred randomly chosen victims, Cian had been the only one to say something as she died. Why was she the only one to leave last words? Were those even "last words," as we like to think of them, or just something she happened to say? My selection had been truly random, and while it had been just a coincidence that Cian's name was on the list, I found it hard to believe that the other ninety-nine people's not saying anything before committing suicide, or even leaving a note, had also been a coincidence.

"Go through all the records and pull out just the ones containing the subject's voice," I told the database. This got me a few results, all mundane snippets of daily conversation with family or friends, none of which seemed connected in any way to the optimal methods of suicide they were about to employ.

I'm sorry, Miach.

Which left Cian Reikado as the exception. The only one with something to say.

That something being the name of the girl who had died, leaving us cowardly deserters behind.

≡

I had returned to that place Miach called the "suburb of the soul." Back to an endless, boring future of connected blocks, their nanomaterial plaster walls painted in light pastels.

I took an automag from the hotel. I didn't care to experience the horror of the subway again, nor did I feel like going back to my own home. I was here to visit Miach Mihie's parents.

I'm sorry, Miach.

I couldn't exactly go to the police or Prime Inspector Os Cara Stauffenberg and tell them that the trigger for 6,582 people across the world taking their lives had been those words—words important only to myself, Cian, and Miach. They wouldn't believe me. In fact, they'd probably recommend me for immediate therapy.

I wasn't sure I would be able to explain why I was going to find Miach's parents. Certainly not because one of 6,582 people had mentioned her name before committing suicide.

Truth be told, I didn't really believe me either. I had come here on the strength of a clue you could barely call a clue, a gut feeling that was hardly reliable enough to call a gut feeling, and an emotion that was something like fear—fear of the ghost of Miach Mihie. In a world where everything was public property, my reason was so private it was almost lewd.

Through the lens of AR, everyone in the world wore their

```
<list:item>
    <i: name>
    <i: age and occupation>
    <i: social assessment score>
    <i: current state of health>
</list>
```

on their sleeve. Focus for any amount of time on someone you saw in the street, and a box of data would appear by their head, telling you everything you could possibly want to know about them. In lifeist society, where it was considered a moral obligation to reveal personal information, especially that concerning one's health, the very word *private* had the illicit stench of secrecy to it.

≡

So it was that I found myself on a solo investigation, using the authority granted me by the Geneva Convention as a Helix agent to the fullest extent. Miach Mihie's parents had moved several months after their daughter died, but it did not take me long to track down their new residence.

The neighborhood was one of those admedistration collectives with security cameras monitoring all passersby. At the entrance to the zone, you had to switch from whatever mode of transport you had used to get there to a collective-provided magcar. I stepped out of the car and walked up to the front door of the house, then pressed my index finger to the fingerplate.

<recollection>
"Hey, Tuan, did you know that people used to hit doors with their hands?"

Miach's voice in my memory.

"There used to be no way to tell who was standing outside your door at all. Some people installed little fisheye lenses on their doors, but that was about the limit of the technology. Not that being in the dark about the people around you was any big deal back then—there weren't ubiquitous personal information displays all the time half a century ago. These days, you just touch the plate on the door and all your info is posted to the AR of the person inside on their wall or something, but they didn't have any way of doing that before."

"So they just hit the door? That's so, I don't know, *primitive*," Cian said.

"It was the easiest way to announce their presence to whoever was inside. They called it 'knocking.' You used your knuckles, like this." Miach demonstrated on the classroom wall. "When a person inside heard the knocking, they would shout out 'Who is it?' and the person on the outside would shout back 'It's so-and-so from such-and-such.' And the person inside just had to take them at their word. So, if you think about it, every time you opened your door, you were taking a little risk."

Cian and I nodded enthusiastically, starry-eyed at the seemingly limitless font of knowledge that was Miach Mihie.

"But you got to think people are getting tired of this telling-everyone-who-they-are-all-the-time business. What a drag it is to have to show you're healthy and you're taking care of yourself all the time. We're tired of it, right? People shouldn't have to walk around with labels over their heads, proving every minute and every second exactly who they are to the world."

"Say, Tuan—"

Another memory.

"You know *privacy* didn't used to be such a naughty word."

I shook my head, eyes flitting around the room. I couldn't believe she had just said that word here in class, in the middle of the day.

Not that Miach ever cared who heard her proclamations.

"It was because," she continued, oblivious, "information about yourself used to be available only to yourself and a few others. That's what *privacy* meant. But now, everything that used to be private is public, so the only thing 'private' these days is sex. Now, why do you think that happened, Cian?"

Cian shrugged her shoulders.

For some reason, a light went off in my head at that moment. "It's like we've offered ourselves to the rest of the world as hostages to guarantee our own good behavior," I said eagerly.

Miach smiled. "That's right, Tuan, it's *just* like that."

I remember feeling a little elation at having said something to please her.

"It's just like Tuan says. By letting everyone else know every little detail about ourselves, we're making sure we can't get away with anything. Give up your erratic free will as a hostage to everyone else in society and you're guaranteed to keep things safe and peaceful."

This was how Miach dispensed wisdom, little by little, to us little girls in the corner of a classroom, explaining to us exactly why we were so frustrated and why we felt like we didn't belong.

Thinking back on it now, I'm amazed it never occurred to me at the time to wonder what sort of people Miach's parents were. I had never met them, and I didn't remember Miach ever talking about them.

Eventually, I had told Miach who my dad was, that he had written the thesis that led to WatchMe, that he had contributed significantly to the world we despised.

All Miach had said was "huh."

She hadn't lost it. She hadn't hated me. She had hardly reacted at all.

`</recollection>`

Now I found I really was curious what kind of parents it took to raise a girl who could smile while she daydreamed out loud about using a household medcare unit to kill fifty thousand people. I removed my finger from the plate and waited quietly for an answer.

"Might I ask what sort of business a member of an international organization has with us?" the door said, breaking the silence and snapping me out of my reverie fully back into the present.

"I'm with the Helix Inspection Agency—I suppose you saw that from my ID. We're an investigative branch of WHO. I was hoping I could talk to you for a moment concerning the multiple suicides in the Sukunabikona Conclave yesterday."

The door opened and a woman emerged. She looked to be in her late fifties. It was Reiko Mihie, Miach's mother.

```
<disappointment>
```
Her face held none of Miach's twisted willfulness, that "dark illumination" for lack of a better term—none of her eccentric vitality. Instead, her face was like that of every other admedistration member, like the people I had seen on the subway upon my return to Japan. They were healthy but lifeless, if that made any sense. Compared to the Kel Tamasheq whose bodies, wrapped in indigo, practically shimmered with a vitality that sprang from their deep history, the people living in this country were like walking corpses.

That's progress, said the Miach Mihie living inside me. The more advanced a people became, the closer they grew to death.
```
</disappointment>
```

"Of course I'm happy to help in any way that I can. I'm just not sure what that would be."

"I wanted to ask you about your daughter, Miach."

A cloud passed over Reiko's face. I saw confusion in her eyes.

"My daughter has been gone—dead—for more than ten years now. I'm sorry, but I don't see the connection."

"Yes, I'm aware of this," I said, marveling that this woman didn't appear to remember her daughter's friend, or that I had taken an oath to kill myself with her. That I had been one of three foolish little girls.

"Actually, I wanted to talk to you about your daughter before her death."

The mother's eyes dropped like she was scanning the depths of her memory, looking for something she'd lost a long time ago. "Well, this is hardly a pleasant story, but when my daughter was a child, she often tried to take her own life. She slashed her wrists on several occasions."

"I'm aware of that too. It's in our records," I lied.

Reiko, I was there with her. I would have followed her all the way down to hell. "I'm also aware," I said, "that she tried to kill herself by eating too much, and then by not eating at all. As though she were trying to damage her own precious body precisely *because* it was so precious."

From the woman's expression I knew I had hit the mark. And it was true. We had tried to die *because* they told us our bodies were a public resource, *because* they kept telling us our bodies didn't belong to us.

"We loved her, truly we did. We wanted her to grow up healthy, to make a contribution to society. But we failed. She was always cleverer than we were by far, and stronger, and yet, at the same time, fragile—a delicate little girl."

"So what happened?"

"It's kind of a long story. Maybe you should come inside," Reiko said, drawing away from the door. She led me into an extremely average living room, motioned for me to sit on a sofa, and disappeared into the kitchen, asking as she went if I liked the smell of lavender. I made some noncommittal grunts, not really having an opinion on the subject.

"Here," she said upon her return and handed me a glass of water. I took it. It did smell like lavender. This was a recent trend—using your medcare unit to add scents to drinking water. It probably had something to do with the whole aromatherapy concept that smells could help generate a feeling of calm.

A good 80 percent of admedistrative society was this: pastel pink buildings and lavender scents.

"So, you tried to help her, and what happened?" I asked Reiko as she sat down across from me. The woman who had once been Miach's mother—I suppose that technically she still was—turned her eyes toward the twisted branches of a palmetto growing outside the window.

"Miach was adopted. Maybe you remember the admedistration campaign to adopt war orphans to counterbalance the problem of our aging society? There were those posters: 'The best resource of all is our youth.' We had tried to have a child of our own, but

I was told by the doctor that my body couldn't produce children. When my husband and I imagined the long lives ahead of us, thanks to WatchMe, just years of gradually growing old, it seemed so...flat, so homogeneous. How horrible, we thought, and how sad. Maybe you remember the conflict in Chechnya?"

I told her it was still going on.

"Is that so? Well, that's where Miach was from. She was the child of a minority group there, a very small community, the admedistration official told us. Their facial features resemble ours quite a lot, and she was only eight years old when we got her, so they told us she wouldn't have any problem getting used to our family and our way of life. All of which was very good news to us. They did mention she'd seen some pretty rough times, but that she'd gone through heavy therapy for her trauma already, and all we needed to do was provide a warm, loving home for her."

    <surprise>
        Miach, a war orphan? I was sure she'd never said anything about that. And neither I nor Cian ever doubted she was Japanese. She spoke fluently, and though she'd had a certain exotic beauty to her features, they fit well within the margins of Japanese variation.
    </surprise>

In the course of my work I'd had several opportunities to meet child soldiers—one of the many scenes AI social filtering kept out of the admedistration media due to a risk of trauma to viewers.

I remembered them in one of the many African countries I visited, carrying the customary AK-47s and a few M-4s from America. Children. Their country was sluggishly transitioning from an antiquated government to an admedistrative system, but there were still armed factions here and there, and the embers of conflict still smoldered.

We were at the negotiation table across from a twelve-year-old boy. A boy who happened to be the leader of an armed force 140 strong—I won't call them "men" because they were boys too. His boys' eyes were blank as they looked over the firepower we were offering them in exchange for their cigarettes and drugs.

Chechnya I'd never been to, but I'd heard plenty of rumors. According to the Helix inspector for the region, the military goods dealer on contract with the Geneva Convention forces there had made a mess of the place with various abuses of the law, only serving to increase the small republic's hatred and distrust of its larger neighbors.

And Miach had been there, in the middle of that tragedy. I knew the crimes that children experienced in war zones. Now I considered the possibility that Miach had seen or experienced many of them herself. For the first time I had learned that Miach was carrying something inside her, a darkness she hadn't told anyone—not even her coconspirators. The fact that she had come from such a hell on earth made her hatred of the admedistrative world—which must have seemed heavenly by comparison—all the more impressive.

"At first she was fine. Everything was normal. But when she got into middle school, it was like she became someone else, possessed almost. She started trying to kill herself. I told you how she attempted to cut her wrists. Well, eventually she found a way to hurt herself without anyone knowing. She came by these drugs—I don't know where—that stopped the body's absorption of nutrition from food. She and some of her friends made a pact that they would kill themselves that way."

<confession>

    I was one of those friends.

    I was that little girl who failed thirteen years ago and hadn't forgotten it for a moment since.

    I and Miach and Cian had taken those pills together in order to strike a blow against the world that had tried to

suffocate us by making us too important to be lost. We wanted to hurt the world, and we were willing to hurt ourselves to do it. Well, some of us, at least.
</confession>

Of course, I said nothing. All I had to do at that point to keep her talking was nod at the appropriate times and occasionally ask a suitably leading question.

"Of course, even when they took the drugs, it still looked like they were eating well. I didn't notice anything. Nor did the parents of the other girls. By the time I did realize something was wrong, Miach had already passed the point of no return."

The woman's eyes fell to her lavender-scented water. "You must think I'm a terrible mother, not to realize my own child was dying before my very eyes."

"No, not at all—"

"No, it's all right. It's the truth, after all." She chewed her lip.

<passion>
"But, I ask you, what can a parent do when their child does something we can't even imagine?" Tears glistened in Reiko Mihie's eyes. "I know that sounds like an excuse, but we really did everything we could to be good parents to her. We went to get advice from the morality center and asked for help from our admedistrative community. The community people were very kind and held several sessions on our behalf."

Was that all you could think of? I thought, cringing inwardly. It was the usual protocol: if a kid had problems, smother them with goodwill until they no longer thought for themselves, or thought anything at all.

Miach didn't have to do much to find herself well beyond the limitations of this woman's small, frail imagination.

"Every time we tried a new approach, Miach seemed to just slip through our hands like sand, drifting off in some

other direction. The pain she was suffering was beyond our ability—no, beyond the whole admedistration's ability to comprehend. She was in pain for reasons we couldn't even imagine, screaming in perfect silence."
</passion>

<disturbed>

To be honest, I hadn't been ready for the woman's pained confession.

Even though, as a Helix agent, I was used to negotiating with admedistrations, the few big governments that refused to die, and the armed factions, I had no tools to deal with this kind of outpouring of raw emotion.

This was the kind of scene you expected in therapy sessions run by the admedistration community and the morality center. The world where everyone knew everything about everyone else. There was no shame in showing your emotions there. Everyone welcomed your grief with a smile and set about debating how to fix things on your behalf. A terrifying thought, I know.

That was the world I had fallen from, hard. The world from which I was estranged.

Confronted with the mother's confession, I realized just how much of an outcast I was from Japan—no, from the entirety of the advanced admedistrative world.
</disturbed>

"I'm sorry. I shouldn't get emotional about this after so much time."

"No, please don't apologize."

Miach's mom shook her head. "I have to. My WatchMe just warned me my emotional state was beyond acceptable parameters for interfacing with others."

"Ah, the public correctness monitoring module?"

"It's a real lifesaver, having another pair of eyes inside me to help me through these things."

A lifesaver, eh? Her WatchMe medicules had been monitoring her pulse and hormonal balance and noticed an aberration in her physical—and therefore mental—state, which it informed her of by sending an alert to her AR contacts. In other words, WatchMe was very subtly guiding not only her body but her mannerisms as well. It was the outsourcing of self-control. We didn't have to worry about our own mental state if we could have something external measure everything for us. The invention of medicules had put the human body and moral precepts side by side on the same lab table.

And here this person was accepting as a perfectly natural part of her daily life the very precepts that Miach had railed against and even felt gratitude for the technology—though for all I knew, she might have secretly abhorred it. The program took signals sent from the body and transmitted morals in return. It was the kind of thing I detested with all my being.

No doubt Miach had felt much the same way.

It was one thing we shared, pure hatred toward the moral code over 80 percent of the people in the world had taken for their own.

"I was going to mention that on my way here, I thought I would stop by Miach's grave and offer her some flowers, but I noticed she hadn't been buried in the family plot. Based on what you've told me, am I right to assume that you returned her remains to Chechnya?"

The mother shook her head and, after taking a moment to compose herself, said, "No. Miach had, on her own initiative, signed a waiver donating her remains to science. It's not such an unusual practice since the Maelstrom."

After that chaotic time of rampant war, cancer, and viruses, the idea that offering your body to science was one of the most admirable things a citizen could do gained wide acceptance, until it was fairly common practice to include a medical donation in your will. Even though not a single governmental law or admedistrative article enforced or even suggested it, the custom to give one's body to science still remained a popular one.

"And you didn't put the liquid reduction of her remains in the grave either?"

"No—we gave those to a certain university professor. And that was her wish too. Someone in that city in the Middle East, the medical bubble place they always talk about, where all the admedistrations have their research labs—"

"You mean Baghdad."

When the nation known as the United States had been the premier global power, back at the beginning of the century, the region around Baghdad had been a festering, war-torn shambles. But now it was like a medical mecca risen from the sands, the place where every medical organization with any clout wanted to have their headquarters.

"Yes, that's the place, Baghdad. A researcher at one of the institutions there specifically requested Miach's remains."

"Could you tell me who this person was?"

"Yes. His name was Mr. Kirie. Nuada Kirie."

```
<silence>
<surprise>
```

I had no idea why my father's name should come up now—my father who had chosen to leave his family for the protective shell of a research laboratory. The doubts that had been troubling me flared into full-blown chaos. Of course, my years of dealing with powerful military men and gangbangers in various unstable regions had taught me not to show fear or confusion on my face, and I didn't now.

Nuada Kirie.

Funny that he had left me and my mother behind to devote himself to his research so soon after my failed attempt to die along with Cian and Miach.

```
</surprise>
</silence>
```

"Why, that's your name too, isn't it? Could he be a relative of yours?"

"Not that I'm aware of. You wouldn't happen to have his contact information, would you?"

"Yes, well, unfortunately I'm unable to contact Mr. Kirie. Something to do with lab security."

"You mean you gave your only daughter's remains to someone and now you can't contact them? Not at all?" I asked, frowning a bit exaggeratedly. It occurred to me that making a show of putting some pressure on this woman might loosen her tongue.

"No, well…" she said.

"You do have a way of contacting him." It wasn't a question.

"Yes, though I was told not to tell anyone."

"Don't worry. I'm an investigator for an international organization. Legally speaking, our authority exceeds that of any medical industrial body."

"Well, Mr. Kirie has an associate here in Japan. A man by the name of Saeki."

Keita Saeki. Another familiar name. Another person I knew.

```
<reference:thesis:id=stid749-60d-r2yrui6ronl>
    <title>
        "Concerning the Possibility of Homeostatic
        Health Monitoring with Medical Particle
        (Medicule) Swarms and Plasticized
        Pharmalogical Particles (Medibase)."
    </title>
    <author>Nuada Kirie, researcher</author>
    <author>Keita Saeki, coresearcher</author>
</reference>
```

03

<recollection>

"So, why were *you* friends with Miach, Cian?"

We were on the sixty-second floor of the Lilac Hills building, waiting for our *insalata di caprese*. Cian seemed surprised by my question at first. Then she was silent, a thoughtful look on her face. I decided to wait patiently for her answer. It took a while, but before too long she nodded as though she had come to some sort of decision.

"You know the thing with the drug, the one that cuts off nutrition. I was the one who ratted us out. I told my parents."

Nothing. No anger. Our suicide pact felt like ancient history by that point, the act of three little girls thirteen years ago, bound together only by a shared hatred of the world. Years later, I could think about it pretty objectively, and I honestly couldn't blame Cian for bailing.

"No kidding."

"You're not angry?"

"Come on, we were kids. It'd take way too much effort to be angry with you now." I smiled and urged Cian to keep talking, not realizing at the time where that conversation would lead.

"Thanks."

"I guess I should thank you. You saved my life."

"No. I betrayed both of you. And I couldn't save Miach."

"You shouldn't carry that one around with you. Don't. I want to hear the rest of this story."

Cian fell silent again. I figured she had a lot of pieces to put together before she could even talk about these things—things she'd probably never told a soul before now.

"See," she said at last, "I stopped taking them, the pills. After only a day or two. I was scared. I felt myself getting thin and weak for the first time. I didn't have WatchMe installed back then of course, none of us did, but my parents had a health consultant that put together a life plan for all of us. The medcare unit kept us in tip-top shape all the time. I mean, I'd never even had a headache at that point."

"Same with me."

"I guess I realized for the first time how much it could hurt to live. I could feel myself alive, and changing. I wasn't eternal or permanent, you know? 'This is life,' I thought. 'This pain is proof I'm alive.' And when I thought that, I got so scared. I have a life, I *am* life."

"I...think I know what you mean."

"That's why I stopped taking the pills. Of course I couldn't tell you or Miach. Which meant I couldn't tell anyone. By the time I realized I had to and went to my parents, it was already too late."

Tears were forming in Cian's eyes. Thirteen years. For thirteen years she'd held all of this inside. How hard that must have been. It wasn't the kind of thing a session or two of therapy could make right.

"Hey, it's not your fault, Cian."

"I know that. I mean, I *should* know that. But I don't."

"Well, it should be enough to know that there's at least one person who's grateful you did what you did, and she's sitting right here. Believe me, I'm *glad* I'm still alive."

"Heh. Okay. Thanks."

"Maybe we should talk about something else."

I was starting to worry. Everything I'd said was the truth. I really was grateful to Cian. I was still alive thanks to her, and being alive meant I could still hurt myself with cigars and tobacco and alcohol. Not that I could say any of that in public.

"No, it's okay. I want to talk about this." Cian wiped away a stray tear and took a deep breath to steady herself. "Looking back on it now, I think I felt like I had to be with Miach. That's why I hung out with her."

"*Had* to be?"

"It's like, I thought of myself as a counterbalance. I was having a tough time with the world back then too, just like you and Miach. I felt suffocated all the time, like I didn't have a place to go. There was just too much, I don't know, *love* in the world, and it was strangling me. They kept telling me what an important resource I was to society and I kept thinking 'No, I'm not. How could that possibly be true?'"

"That's what Miach always said, wasn't it. 'We aren't resources! We have to prove we don't have any value at all!'"

Cian nodded. "Yeah, and I agreed with her, I really did—but I didn't think that meant we had to kill somebody or die ourselves. For all that Miach and I saw eye to eye, I couldn't follow her all the way to that conclusion. But when I looked at Miach, I knew she could. I knew she'd go right up to the edge."

"So you thought you would balance that. I get it."

"That's right. I thought if I was there with her, I could hold her back. I could keep Miach from going too far. I would just listen to everything she said, and nod, and agree, and it would be enough for her just to have an audience, you know? She wouldn't actually have to *do* any of the things she always talked about. Of course, it didn't work out like that. In the end I was just a coward, and Miach was dead."

I felt like I had, for the first time, touched a little of the pain this woman must have carried inside her for the last thirteen years. *I think I know what you mean*, I'd told her. I didn't know shit. The pain Cian had carried was deep, harsh, and she had carried it all alone for more than a decade.

Cian hadn't been a hanger-on. I'd had her all wrong. She had been stronger than any of us, and more noble, and more alone. All alone.

Miach and I, we were little girls, but Cian Reikado had been an adult.

"That's amazing, Cian. I could never have been that strong."

She shook her head. "I wasn't strong. I was too scared to do anything else."

Cian leaned back, the view from the sixty-second floor of the Lilac Hills building stretching out behind her, as the waiter arrived carrying sliced tomatoes and mozzarella cheese on two white plates.

"*Caprese*'s here," Cian said. "It's been a long time since we ate together."

```
</recollection>
```

≡

They closed the lid on Cian's coffin while the procession watched.

As was the custom, the family had chosen a gentle, light pink for the coffin. Like they could paint over the horrible, illogical shock of losing someone so abruptly in an age when everyone was supposed to live forever. Most of the people in the procession wore light yellow and emerald green in mourning. The ceremony had been brief. Cian's cold body would now be carried by hearse to the local reduction facility. I watched the family procession leave the community center. I had no desire to go to the factory. I didn't think I'd be able to stand there and wait for the reduction process to finish. I was out of time as it was. I had to figure out why Cian had died before they dragged me off to therapy.

The factory, the melting pot, the reduction center.

It was a relic from the time of the mutant viruses after the nukes dropped.

The bodies of the dead were reduced with a protein liquefier, and the resulting goop was further processed to remove any possibility of viral or bacterial transmission. The processing plant of the dead. A reminder of more chaotic times that had lived on for over half a century now. From a law-enforcement perspective, it was a pain in the ass. You couldn't use medicules to analyze someone's brain once it'd been liquefied.

Back during the Maelstrom, when mutant plagues ran rampant, corpses were nothing more than disease vectors to be eliminated as quickly as possible. Corpses started new outbreaks, and merely scorching the flesh wasn't enough. The custom that arose under those conditions became the norm, which meant that bodies these days were dealt with as soon as possible. After an extremely brief autopsy to determine cause of death, the body would be subjected to protein reduction and that was it.

While it was still possible to use imaging to examine a corpse after the fact, there was no time to use medicules to investigate anything on the nano level.

<sentiment>

"Goodbye, Cian. And thank you," I muttered toward the hearse as it drove away from the funeral home. A soft breeze against my face was Cian's answer. I felt like crying for a little while after that, but I stood and watched the car until I could no longer see it. Our friend. She had watched over us. She had saved my life. And she had suffered for it for years.

Maybe she was the kind of comrade-in-arms Miach had been looking for.

To me, Cian Reikado had been a friend.

A little girl, braver than any of us, and more of an adult than I would ever be.

</sentiment>

I wiped away a tear with the back of my hand and left the funeral home to go to the university where Keita Saeki worked. While Nuada Kirie, aka my father, had gone off to Baghdad, his partner had remained behind to continue his research here in Japan. He was still at the same school where he and my father had worked together on their medicule theories so many years before.

≡

I parked my car in the university lot and touched my hand to the screen of a FindYou on the way into the school (the granite base that the screen sat on gave it a nice academic look) and announced I was looking for Keita Saeki. The message SEARCHING appeared in the middle of the screen as the FindYou hunted for Keita's WatchMe signal. After a moment, the lab and a map showing how to get there rose up on the screen. I touched the display to transfer the map to my own AR, and willfully ignoring the looks that my crimson Helix agent uniform got from the students, I followed the bobbing arrows that appeared in the air in front of me toward the laboratory.

Past a row of evergreens with pink leaves I found the building I was looking for. I pressed a finger to the door to identify myself and made for the laboratory.

"Come on in, I've been waiting for you," came a familiar voice from inside. Of course, when I'd asked the FindYou to locate him, it let Keita Saeki know (as was his legal right) that I was looking for him. I strode through the door into the cluttered office.

"Wow, what a mess."

The place was a mountain of printouts—manuscripts and research materials and the like. There were mounds of other dead media too. The thin black squares I recognized as floppy disks. "They're like memorycels," he had told me once when I had visited the laboratory as a child. As for the other things there, I had no idea what they might be called. Just looking at them, it was hard to even imagine what they might do.

"I'm surprised you can even walk around in here," I said, making a show of hopping from bare spot to bare spot, going toward the professor like someone jumping from rock to rock across a river.

"I manage. Besides, ThingList remembers where I put everything if I ever need to find it," the professor replied as he scratched his tangled monkey-puzzle-tree of a hairdo with one hand.

"It's not a question of practicality. It's a question of mental hygiene."

"For scientists it's *always* a question of need, Miss Kirie. As long as my ThingList has location tags, and it does, there's no need for me to remember where anything is. I can just follow the arrows."

"ThingList is a bad influence."

"I like to think of it as outsourcing my memory to someone far more competent. I use a NeedList inside my ThingList so I don't forget anything when I go out either."

"Well, I spend a lot of time off-line, so that wouldn't work for me."

"Where's that thesis?" Keita addressed the room. "The one that Czech mathematician wrote three years ago." A long, pink, rubbery appendage extended from the intelligent material on the ceiling, moved about thirty feet across the room, then grew fingers to fish several sheets of a printout from a large stack, which it then brought to us. Everything in the room was tagged for identification and immediate retrieval—which meant that somewhere on the university server there was a perfect real-time replica of the professor's office. No wonder the human race was growing soft.

I stood next to the professor and a gelatin seat materialized from the floor beneath me.

"Care for some water?"

"Got any caffeine?"

"Nah. The university—that is the student admedistration— won't allow it. I'm surprised how well this generation looks after itself."

"Wasn't it your generation that wanted society to be this way?"

"Now now, how could anyone have predicted such an extremely health-conscious society would rise out of what we had before? Yo, two waters please."

Once again the arm extended from the ceiling, pouring water into two cups and carrying them to us.

"There are many from our generation that can't bear to fit into the molds society stamps for them," I told him. "Plenty of people in your generation too, for that matter."

"Give birth, consume. That's the safe, stable cycle of life. Those who would attempt to destroy themselves, and thereby destroy that cycle, are anathema to the rest of us. Before they are allowed to do such a thing, it is our responsibility to notice the telltale signs and subject them to heavy therapy. That's what being a thoughtful society means."

"Don't you think we've reached the limits of our over-considerate society by now?"

"What we've reached is a healthy, conflict-free status quo. Though the statistical rise in suicides within admedistrative society is troubling for sure, there are many who believe that pharmaceuticals and the development of novel therapeutic treatments, as well as the legal support for such treatments, will eventually bring the trend under control."

"You seem well, professor."

"Show me someone who doesn't. With disease virtually abolished, it shouldn't be hard. A lot of old expressions have lost their teeth that way, you know."

Colds.

Migraines.

Infectious diseases.

I wondered how much pain I would have to feel before I could truly prove I existed. That I felt pain. That I was satisfied.

Cian had felt pain, and it terrified her.

She was frightened of being an undeniably living creature, with a nervous system and the whole works.

It went a little differently for the elderly. Life span was a hard out and an undeniable barrier. The older you got, the more you experienced that balance between life and death, and the more you began to fall apart, beyond the abilities of WatchMe and a medcare unit to catch up.

"Speaking of losing teeth, you can't say that a feeble old man has no health problems," I challenged him.

"True enough. There is no panacea for old age, I'll give you that. But you have to agree those little buggers your dad and I cooked up are doing one hell of a job."

"Well, for a world without disease, people sure do spend a lot of time gabbing about their health."

The professor shrugged his shoulders as if to say *it's no fault of mine*. He moved dexterously for a man in his mid-eighties.

"That's because everyone's still afraid that all it will take is one misstep and the cancers and viruses will be right back on us."

"It's already been half a century since the Maelstrom."

"And the people who had to live through that—myself included—have control of the admedistrations. Plenty of councilors and commissioners are in their seventies and eighties. That chaos and the nuclear war that followed made our world a very harsh environment. The kind of place where you'd die without a space suit on. It was like living in a space station, one thin wall away from oblivion. The nuclear war and the radiation it spread made the perpetuation of our species a very dicey proposition, which it still would be without the help of homeostatic monitoring thanks to WatchMe and constant treatment by a medcare unit. You need strong armor to live in a harsh world."

"So, even though the radiation's gone, the fear remains?"

"Well, there's a lot to be said for socialistic tendencies. Did you know that the first group to attempt the nationwide eradication of cancer and the prohibition of smoking were the Nazis?"

Fleeting memories of twentieth century history as taught in school.

With the Maelstrom waiting at the end of the semester, the sorry fate of the twentieth century Jews got sidelined in class. The longer history got, the more compressed its parts became.

"We'll be lucky if we get one minute's time," Miach had said once. Leave it to Miach to imagine a history lesson one thousand years in the future. And who wouldn't want to skip such an uneventful period in favor of something more exciting?

As history marched on, our time would shrink, and shrink, and shrink away until finally there'd be nothing left.

The tragic genocide of the Jews was hanging on, tooth and nail, to its two minutes in class.

"They're the lot who killed all those Jews, right?"

"You make them sound like rabble. They were a nation. Democratic in origin, with citizens, and voting, and a representative government. The Nazis took control over the details of daily life to a greater extent than anyone before them. They made a register of all cancer patients, listing all who had been affected, categorizing and analyzing them, all in the first organized attempt to eradicate cancer in history."

"Fascism, was it? The political system in Germany under the Nazis, I mean."

"Yes, and you can draw clear parallels between our admedistrative system and the health policies of the Nazis, if you like. Were you aware that pejorative words like *fatty* dropped from our language over the last half century?"

"Actually, I did know that one." I chuckled. *Miach Mihie, banzai!*

"Under Nazi rule, the 'crippled' became the 'physically impaired.' Lunatic asylums became psychiatric hospitals. Countless words pertaining to the human body changed in subtle ways."

"What's *lunatic* mean?"

"Think of it as a not-very-nice way to refer to someone in serious need of high-level counseling and deep therapy. The Nazis also spearheaded the first nationwide attempt to stamp out smoking because of its detrimental effects on health. In 1939, the Nazi government established a regulatory agency for alcohol and tobacco products. In 1941, a research laboratory to study the harmful effects of tobacco was established at the Universität Wien under the auspices of Hitler himself."

"You make it sound like the Nazis were a bunch of do-gooders."

With these cherry-picked examples, Nazi society didn't sound all that different from ours. Which meant that now I had a personal reason to hate the Nazis as the forebears of the assholes who wouldn't let me smoke today.

"In a sense, that's true. Even if they were responsible for the greatest genocide of the twentieth century. There are many sides to everything, that's the point. Take a clean freak and turn them up a few notches, whammo, they're talking about racial purity. 'Tobacco is the source of all ills, a danger to the nation's citizens.' That's a protoform of what we call resource awareness today."

I shrugged. "So we've just reinvented Nazi Germany on a global scale then. Great."

"In a sense, yes, we have. Though there are significant differences. Foremost among them is that, in the time of the Nazis, it was the Nazi party and a few scientists who were pushing eugenics as a way to clean things up. In admedistrative society, everyone's out there together, waving the same flag. We are all health freaks. The Nazis might have had the idea long before us, but not even they could keep their own soldiers on the front lines from smoking—especially in the harsher places like the Eastern Front."

"Oh, I understand that. I really understand that." I chuckled. Of course, for me it worked the other way around. It wasn't battlefield conditions that made me smoke. It was the smokes that lured me out to the battlefield. I wondered for the first time what had become of Étienne and the others who used to partake in our contraband exchanges. For a moment, I was transported back to the sunflower fields and blue skies of the Sahara, dotted with the indigo veils of the Kel Tamasheq.

"But now tobacco's gone from the world. Save for a few holdouts in Africa and parts of Asia—conflict zones, mostly. Go to any admedistration and you'll not find a single constituent partaking of either cigarettes or alcohol. The same goes without saying for harder drugs. Do you know why drugs were prohibited in the first place, way back when?"

"Enlighten me."

"It started back during the settlement of North America. The slaves and laborers brought in from Africa and China had a custom of chewing on coca leaves, which enabled them to work far beyond the usual limits of their physical bodies. Of course, this didn't amuse the white laborers who weren't partaking. By abolishing drugs for moral reasons, they attempted to wrest the title of top laborers from so-called inferior races."

"That's funny. I always thought it was because drugs ruined people's lives."

"Well, that's true too, but that's only one aspect of the truth." The professor leaned back in his chair. "Of course, my generation is blessed and cursed with having seen the reasons why our current health-obsessed society needs to be what it is. And I'm sure you had to sit through your share of lessons on the Maelstrom when you were in school, Tuan."

The section of history class dealing with the Maelstrom was a curriculum heavyweight. Thinking back on it, it occurred to me that history had always been Miach's favorite subject—the only one she was truly passionate about—and the Maelstrom was her favorite part of that.

I had never been much interested in history class, even though we were always happy to receive Miach's gleanings of wisdom from the same.

Hey, Tuan, you know what?

A whole ten million people died during just a few years in North America...

"That's mostly because the people writing your textbooks were just the right age to remember the Maelstrom with fear," Professor Saeki went on. "There were riots all over America—the strongest and wealthiest nation in the world at the time—that touched every corner of the land. A lot of racial cleansing too. Hispanics, Koreans, Africans—everyone was a target. The killing was so frenzied you would think everyone in the country had been born with an organ specifically designed for massacring people who didn't look like them. So ethnicity killed ethnicity, and the chaos spread to other countries, until the terrorists decided to start lobbing the nukes they'd stolen, and everything went to hell. Our current benevolent society is a reaction to that. Some people might find the air a bit stifling, but it's a sight better than falling into chaos like the Maelstrom again. After all, no one wants to see themselves and their children die, and what we have now is far preferable to the past, when a few men in smoke-filled rooms had all the power."

"I'm glad we've learned how to tame each other, then. It's like we're all one another's pets, isn't it."

"Always a cynic. Look, when people experience something really extreme, it's very difficult for them to find balance after that. Their reaction usually points in an equally extreme opposite direction. That's how we got our lifeist society. I agree, we've gone overboard for sure. It's a bit silly to keep a piggy bank around when your wallet's always full—but you wouldn't know what a piggy bank is, would you, Tuan?"

I tried to keep from laughing out loud and only mostly succeeded.

The professor raised an eyebrow at me. "Something funny?"

"No, I was just remembering having heard a friend use that expression a long time ago."

"You don't say." The professor shrugged. "Whatever, I'm sure you didn't come here to learn about antiquated idiomatic expressions. What do you want to know, Tuan? When a WHO agent comes calling, it's usually something important."

"Miach Mihie."

It was quick, but I didn't miss the look of alarm that passed across Professor Saeki's eyes. He put one hand to his mouth and looked thoughtful. "Hmm, yes. I received her body on Nuada's behalf."

"Where is my father?"

"A good question. Neither of us have tried contacting each other for quite some time."

I decided I would press the attack. "My father took Miach along with him to Baghdad, didn't he?"

The professor waved his hand as if to suggest this was not a fruitful line of questioning. The old man's guard was up, I could tell.

"Where is my father? Is he not in Baghdad?"

The professor shook his head and sighed. "If he's not in Baghdad, then your guess is as good as mine. Why not ask the global FindYou?"

"I did. Apparently, he's no longer on the planet."

He cocked his head. "What do you suppose that means?"

"I didn't get a single hit from a search. Nor is he on any of the death records of any admedistration. He might've turned off the location signal on his WatchMe, but even then I'd still get a hit—I just wouldn't know where he was."

I stared at the professor, wondering how many of his defenses I would have to patiently dismantle, how many moats I would have to fill to get to the truth. No wonder Miach's mother gave me his contact information, for all the good it was doing me.

Professor Saeki scratched his head and chewed his lip. "That's perplexing. Mind telling me why the sudden interest in finding your father?"

"Actually, I'm not that interested in my father. What I want to know is what happened to Miach. You're aware of the mass suicide the other day?"

"Over six thousand people across the planet killed themselves at exactly the same time. Show me someone who doesn't know about it."

"Well, I think Miach Mihie was involved, and before you remind me, yes, I know she's been dead for thirteen years."

Keita Saeki was silent. A hard look came into his eyes. "If that's what you want to know about, you should talk to the woman who was working as Nuada's assistant in Baghdad. Name of Gabrielle Étaín. She's in the Baghdad labs of the SEC neuromedical consortium. Nuada and Gabrielle worked there together."

"What were they working on?"

"Do you really need to know?" he asked. I could see his mind racing behind his eyes.

"I'll be the judge of that. If I have to, I can get a warrant from the Japanese police."

The professor stared at me, his mouth hanging slightly open. This wasn't my first time at the negotiation table, and I wasn't going to let some eccentric scholar locked up in his ivory tower talk me out of getting the information I wanted.

"It seems as though Nuada's daughter has only grown wilder with age."

"It's an occupational disease. There are worse symptoms, if you care to see them."

"That's quite all right. I frighten easily enough," the professor said. He called up a command pad on his desktop screen and began downloading data from someplace. He indicated the desk, so I reached out and touched it to do the transfer.

A densely packed scientific paper began scrolling at high speed through my AR.

"I don't have time to read all this and you know it."

"Call it my little way of getting back at you."

"Um, excuse me?"

"I'm kidding, mostly. Let me sum it up for you. The paper is concerned with human will. A certain Russian researcher was able to use a psychological simulation based on these data to create a fairly detailed model of how the human will works."

The professor pulled up a 3-D image embedded in the paper. It was a small picture of the brain that now began to rotate in my AR. A narrow wedge of it was blinking.

I pointed. "What's that?"

"Part of the mesencephalon, the midbrain," he said. "This is the part that governs the feedback system in our brains. Put simply, it processes the signals that motivate us to do things. Every action, no matter how small, has its associated reward. In most cases it's a simple sensation of pleasure or fulfillment. If I have sex I will feel good—that's a very simple, extreme example. Actually, my explanation is slightly off, but all you need to know is the general concept here. What I'm talking about is the range of feedback, great and infinitesimally small, that inspires us to repeat certain choices. This reward system creates a vast variety of motivating desire modules that compete for our attention. We call the act of choosing between these modules our *will*."

The professor looked at me as if to ask whether I understood. I motioned for him to continue.

"Picture, say, a conference room. Real or in an AR session, it doesn't matter. There're all these people there and they're all clamoring for this or that, until they boil things down to a collection of salient points and come to a conclusion. Think of the desire modules we all carry around as the people in that meeting, trying to get their opinions heard. When we think of human will, it's common sense to think of it as a single existence or an all-discerning soul. But it's not. It's the heated debate, the shouting and the name-calling. It's the process itself. The will isn't one thing, it's all of your desires clamoring for attention—that very state of being. Humans forget that we are a collection of disparate fragments and go around calling ourselves 'I' as though we were one immutable entity. It's comical, really."

"And this paper models that system?"

The professor dropped his display and leaned forward on his desk, nodding. "It does. When Nuada read this, he realized that if you could influence the various elements in a person's feedback system, you could influence their will. Even control it."

Controlling a person's will?

I appreciated the professor's finesse in saying something of such dire import with all the nonchalance of someone discussing the weather.

"Desire is very closely linked to reward. If the reward associated with a particular desire is slight, it reduces our will to act on that desire, and it becomes very hard for that particular desire to take the floor in that meeting of modules I talked about. People change their minds all the time. It's the differences in reward levels that change our will, and it's all mapped out. We even know how the feedback system interacts with different parts of the brain. The only problem was creating the medicules that could act on this knowledge. There needed to be a way to get the troops into the battlefield, which is the midbrain in this case."

A light went on in my head. "Past the blood-brain barrier."

"There is that, yes. But that's only one of the problems involved. In any case, that's what Nuada went to Baghdad to study."

Controlling people's desires.

Controlling people's wills.

If you could sweep up all the fragments that made up our souls and lock them together like pieces of a puzzle, could you make a perfect person? What kind of person would that be?

Not someone like Miach. Not someone like me.

Miach had implored us to show our lack of value to the world. The day they figured out how to completely control a person's will, the point would be moot.

I pictured a world of people all living together in perfect harmony.

A perfect society, run by perfect people, perfectly.

Our collective medical society was a good start in that direction. All it lacked was the tool sufficient to finish the job. My father had left myself and my mother and Japan to go to Baghdad to find that tool. To fashion a scalpel sharp enough to cut souls.

"Don't take this the wrong way, Tuan, but the prospect of being able to fiddle with a person's soul makes for a very attractive research project."

The professor scratched his head, averting his eyes from me, as though he felt he shared a bit of my father's guilt. His gaze drifted to the row of pink-leaved trees outside the window. "You can't wave a good idea like this in front of a scientist and expect them not to reach for it. I'm not condoning what he did to you and your mother, but I'd be lying if I said I didn't understand what it's like to be a scientist in his position—and why he left you to go to Baghdad."

"I understand what you're saying, professor. But you're not my father. His sin is his and no one else's."

I looked away, my eyes wandering until they found a yellow square among the floppy disks scattered across the floor. There was a label on the front of it with some kind of logo and an illustration like one from a children's book. Probably some kind of game in its day.

"Someday, that will be us lying there," the professor said quietly.

I looked up, not understanding.

"Dead media. Relics of a bygone age." He leaned back in his chair. "You've read those science fiction stories where humans manage to digitize the consciousness and upload themselves to some computer network. We do that, and our bodies will be nothing but antiquated dead media as far as our souls are concerned. It's not hard to imagine a few soulless bodies lying around between the piles of magnetic tape and flash memory cards in my office once we evolve our consciousness beyond the need for the flesh."

"Really?" I asked. "I always thought it was the other way around. That the soul was just a function of the body—a means to keep it alive. Once our bodies find something more suitable to propagate themselves and are able to trade in these old souls, then it's we who become the dead media."

That caught him off his guard. The professor sat with a blank expression on his face for a few moments. Then he laughed out loud. "True enough! A very radical idea at first blush, but from the perspective of evolution, I'd say yours is more correct. Perhaps it is I who was caught up in an antiquated notion of the human soul as something sacred and unique."

"The question is, if someone developed the technology to control and change human will, what would they do with it?"

"Tuan." The professor shook his head. "I think, and this is just my opinion, but I think that most scientists don't do research like that with any kind of objective. They aren't thinking what they want to do with it. The research itself is the goal. It's a challenge. Like the mountain climber says, they do it because it's there. If there is an issue of scientific interest, they'll look into it. That's all the motivation they need."

I stood and strode toward the door, not even bothering to pick my way through the piles of printouts that scattered in my wake. I stopped just before I reached the door and said over my shoulder, "Professor, I'm looking for Miach Mihie. Finding my father is just a means to that end."

I left the lab behind me, feeling like I was getting closer to the truth than I had ever been. I could feel it in my bones. I was on the right path.

```
<list:item>
    <i: Miach Mihie>
    <i: my dad>
    <i: consciousness manipulation>
</list>
```

I didn't need bobbing AR arrows to find my way on this one.

≡

Prime Inspector Os Cara Stauffenberg was not pleased with my failure to report my findings either to the Japanese police or to my own Helix Inspection Agency branch. She was on my HeadPhone right now, criticizing me in sentences carefully worded to avoid any offensive language.

"Don't worry, I'm making progress," was all I could tell her, which she followed by asking for more details. Her persistence made me feel like I had somehow unconsciously uttered the shocking words *It's private* and now she had it in for me. Of course, that was just my imagination working overtime. Os Cara had no idea of my growing personal involvement in the investigation.

I walked, letting my eyes wander along the ground, grunting noncommittal replies to her questions as I made my way down the white walkway that led past the pink trees on the way to the university parking lot.

"I'm going to Baghdad."

"What?!"

Though her voice was as smooth as ever, it was clear she was fuming just beneath the surface. Still, she managed an almost civil "Why Baghdad?" to which I replied, "Because that's where my investigation is leading me. Neither of us has a whole lot of options when it comes to what we can say, do we?" I added. That really rubbed her the wrong way.

"Don't think you can keep playing the Niger card over and over again."

"Oh," I said, "I intend to use that one till it's worn around the edges." I stared at the alias graphic my AR displayed in place of Os Cara's real face. It amused me that our aliases looked so calm while we were down in the trenches, lobbing verbal grenades at each other.

Most people had the habit of looking down at their feet while they were on their HeadPhone—probably because otherwise they would get too caught up in the conversation and trip on something. It was such a common sight these days that hardly anyone paid it a second thought, but if someone from a hundred years ago slipped into our time, they would see a bunch of people walking around staring down at the ground muttering to themselves and rightly determine we were all in need of therapy.

I'm sorry, Miach.

Those words tickled the back of my mind. Something about the way Cian had been staring down at her *caprese*. In all the other AR archive footage of the suicides I'd seen, the act had progressed smoothly from what came before. People were just doing whatever they normally did, then they were finding a way to kill themselves.

Cian was the only one who had taken any time before the act, her head bowed, as though she were reflecting on what she was about to do.

She had been the only one to look down, just as I was looking down right now while I talked to Prime Inspector Os Cara Stauffenberg. Just Cian Reikado. Just her.

"Prime, we're going to have to continue this from the PassengerBird. Something really important's just come up."

I cut the call before Prime had time to really lose her shit, and drawing on the access to local police records we Helix agents had been given as part of this investigation, I called up Cian Reikado's phone records.

```
<silence>
```
    The day of Cian's death. 13:16.

    Just before she died.

    As she looked down at her plate.

```
<fear>
```
    My spine froze. That day, as Cian sat across from me staring at her *caprese*, she had been on the phone with someone else.

    I didn't have to think too hard to figure out who it was. Cian had said her name, after all.

    It was just hard to accept.

    It was terrifying to accept.

    A dead person—or at least, someone I had believed to be dead—calling my friend just before her own death. The record of that call from 13:16 two days ago blinked in the corner of my AR, quietly yet steadily demanding that I play back this message from beyond the grave.

```
</fear>
```
    With trembling fingers, I reached out and pressed the blinking entry on the list.

    A voice recording opened.

```
</silence>
```

```
<log:phonelink:id=4ids8094bnuj8hjndf6>
```

Hello, Cian.

Long time no see. Thirteen years, huh?

I'm calling because I wanted to talk to you about what it means to be "good."

I'm talking Good *with a capital* G.

What do you think it means?

It's not about helping people in need or making friends or not hurting others. Those are aspects of being good, but they're really just details. If you get right down to it, Good *is the will it takes to maintain a certain set of values over time.*

That's right, maintenance. Maintaining a family, maintaining happiness, maintaining peace. It doesn't really matter what you're maintaining. All you have to do is keep something going that people believe in. That's the essence of Good.

But nothing goes on forever, does it?

That's why you have to make a constant, conscious effort to be good. You have to keep those branches spreading toward the sun. Good has to be actively maintained. Put it another way, that which you consciously believe in and maintain is Good. Even though that could be all kinds of things.

Too bad our bodies aren't built for the task. People grow, then grow old. People get sick. People die. There's no good or bad in nature because everything always changes. Everything goes away in the end. That's what's kept Good from swallowing up the world so far. That's what's kept people from growing arrogant with all the Good they've done, though only just barely. But now, thanks to WatchMe and medicules, disease and even regular aging are in the process of being eliminated. The value we call health is trampling over everything else. What do you think that means? It means that the flood is coming. We're about to drown.

If it isn't all Good now, it soon will be.

```
</log>
```

It was, beyond a shadow of a doubt, Miach Mihie's voice. It was also, beyond question, her thinking.

```
<log:phonelink:id=4ids8094bnuj8hjndf6:playtime:2
m52s06ms>
```

There've never been so many people governed by Good.

There've never been so many people giving themselves up to Good.

There have been many versions of Good throughout the ages.

When the Bastille fell in France, when the sons of freedom threw crates of tea into the harbor in Boston—every age has had its heroes who try to do Good. That was the whole idea behind America, with its freedom and democracy for all.

But never has Good held so many people's lives in thrall at any one time.

Back when kings ruled, the king would threaten to sentence anyone who turned against him to death, so people listened. They made people obey through violence. That's why the French Revolution was a success. All they had to do was take out the king. Once you have enough people come out and claim a mandate, saying "This is the people's will," all you needed next was violence to finish the job. But with the birth of democracy, rule ceased to come from the top. Now it came from the people. Eventually it got to the point we're at now, where everybody governs themselves.

What do we do if the enemy we're fighting against is inside each of us?

Our lifeism is the ultimate expression of rule by all, and its final destination.

Ever hear of The Three Musketeers? *It's a story—a novel written by Alexandre Dumas—about these three soldiers living in seventeenth century France. In it, there's a saying: "One for all, and all for one."*

That worked fine for them, seeing as how they were only saying it to a couple other people.

In the world of resource awareness, we're making that same oath, except we're swearing it to everyone in our admedistration—no, everyone in the world—and we are expected to surrender our lives to ensure we follow through.

You were supposed to come with me, Cian. You and Tuan. But you didn't.

You said you would fight with me. That we'd fight together. You hurt me. You made me very sad.

But I think if you can show me your courage now, that will be enough. Show the world there's nothing permanent. Show the world your body belongs to you alone. Show everyone right now, and it will be just like it was back in the day.

Back when we were us.

Please, Cian. I need you to be brave.

Show it to me. Show it to the world.

```
</log>
```

My mouth moved, forming Cian's final words along with her. *I'm sorry, Miach.*

```
</body>
</etml>
```

<part:number=03:title=Me, I'm Not/>

```
<?Emotion-in-Text Markup Language:version=1.2:enc
oding=EMO-590378?>
<!DOCTYPE etml PUBLIC :-//WENC//DTD ETML 1.2
transitional//EN>
<etml:lang=jp>
<etml:lang=en>
<body>
```

01

One thing the declaration achieved was to make everyone in the world shut up for a moment. What were you doing when you heard it?

It was cloudy in this city that day. This city being the capital of Japan.

The clouds hung heavy, gray lumps in the sky over the city, waiting to crush the people who braved the streets. Or maybe I was seeing symbolism in everything due to shock.

Reports said some people got sick just hearing it. Many more reported for immediate therapy. When I heard it, I was in my car driving toward the airport with a passenger—the man with the business cards.

```
<recollection>
```
"Ever heard of a business card?"

We were sitting in the classroom during recess time when Miach showed us a small piece of paper.

It was rectangular, small enough to fit in the palm of your

hand, and there were words on it: our school name, our class number, and in larger text below that, MIACH MIHIE.

"Check it out. People used to use these to introduce themselves."

Cian grunted with interest and leaned forward to look at the paper where it lay atop Miach's desk.

"Can't write much of a profile on that little thing, can you?"

Miach nodded. "That's right. And there's no link to your SA score or medical info either. The main social unit back in the day used to be your company or school, so you wrote that address here on the card. In fact, most people didn't even use business cards outside of company interactions. There was no need or means to display personal information at other times."

"Why not?"

"Because privacy was so important back then."

"*Privacy*?" Cian giggled. "Miach, you dog!"

"They didn't have AR like we do, y'know. There were physical limitations to how much information you could get out there."

"That's true," I said, adding so that Cian could understand, "You would've had to walk around with a big sign around your neck if you wanted to do what we do today."

Cian frowned. "But don't people kind of roll their eyes at you if you don't display your creds? Was everyone just shadier back then? And, like, suspicious of each other?"

"No, it's just that you didn't share your personal information with people like you do now. If you were out in public and someone sat down next to you, you didn't pay them any attention. Business cards were for when you were obliged to exchange some limited amount of information, and you had to give them to someone else by hand, so it was more targeted than the indiscriminate spray of information we have now."

"It's kind of cute," I said, picking up the little scrap of paper.

Miach grinned. "Isn't it? I think it's way more cute *and* classy than some AR profile hanging over your head. I knew you'd like it, Tuan."

"Neat, it's even got a picture!" Cian said, pointing at the colorful illustration on the card. "Did you draw that, Miach? What is it, some kind of symbol?"

"Yeah. It's our symbol."

"*Our* symbol?"

"Yeah. For our trio of comrades. You, me, and Tuan."

`</recollection>`

I still had the handmade business card Miach had given me that day in my desk at home. In fact, knowing what a business card was had come in handy once or twice in my work as a Helix agent. I realized that this ancient form of information transfer, completely lost from lifeist society, was still highly valued in negotiations between old-style governments and nations. The Helix agent charged with negotiating cease-fires between the many armed groups in Chechnya and the government in Russia told me that once when he'd produced a business card during a sit-down with one armed group, they'd immediately warmed to him. In places where AR wasn't yet a part of daily life, the culture of business cards still thrived.

I was remembering all this because of the man who ran up to me in the university parking lot as I was getting into my car and handed me his card.

"Agent Elijah Vashlov, Interpol."

I took the card from his hand with practiced ease. Agent Vashlov's eyes widened. "You know what that is?"

"It's not a business card?"

I glanced at the paper. There was nothing cute about a business card received from a strange man who ran up to you in a parking lot. Nothing cute at all. Besides, with a clear AR display showing me who the guy was anyway, there was no need for business cards, which made this all just a parlor trick.

"I'm familiar with the old custom."

"Oh, well that's no fun."

"I hope you don't do that to everyone you meet."

"Actually," he replied, "I do. Most of them rather like it."

Vashlov scratched his head sheepishly. He was clearly fond of performance. I asked him what his business was. I'm not made of time, you know.

"How about we talk in your car. We can just drive around."

"Sorry, but I'm on my way to the airport." I indicated my car with a jab of my jaw.

"Off to Baghdad, right?"

I stared into the man's eyes, taking care to hide my surprise. His face betrayed no emotion, though it was clear he'd been trying to catch me off my guard, which meant I was irritating him. That made me glad.

"That's just what I want to talk to you about," Vashlov said, his words cool and measured. "Just let me go with you and talk to you on the way to the airport. That's all I ask. I won't slow you down."

After a moment's hesitation I nodded, and Vashlov told his own car to go home on its own. I got in and set the route, which brought up a display of the predicted time it would take to get to the airport.

"You've got one hour," I told him.

"More than enough," Vashlov said, getting in next to me.

Something didn't feel right as we drove through the city streets. Maybe it was the heavy clouds overhead, but something seemed to have added a generous dollop of loneliness to the flat landscape of the city. I stared out the window, trying to dig the source of that loneliness out of the passing scenery with my eyes. I was no more enlightened by the time the car reached the entrance to the expressway and we left the streets behind.

Even the expressway seemed unusually vacant that day. *What is it?* I wondered.

It's you. You're lonely, the loneliness answered me.

"With this little traffic, we might get there early," Vashlov said. Then more quietly he added, "They're all afraid, you know."

"Of what?"

"Of someone dying right in front of their eyes. Afraid it might be them."

That made sense.

I'd heard the therapists were overwhelmed.

How could someone just die, right in front of you?

Forced belief in others was what kept our society running. That was what it meant to take a little bit of everyone around you hostage. In exchange for lives that, save for rare accidents, would never end before their time, we were expected to always keep personal information on display, to participate in admedistration discussions and morality sessions, and to make decisions only after receiving advice from the appropriate expert.

But the gears in the clockwork had warped a little bit after the suicides. Though it had happened in a strange way, the "incident" as people were calling it had reminded them of an old familiar feeling—that others were *strangers*. That they were unpredictable and often distasteful.

True enough. If normally stable people were capable of committing suicide at the drop of a hat, it was impossible to know whom you could trust. What would happen if they took their own lives the very moment you did decide to trust them? What would that do to you?

I knew what it had done to me. Eternity had crumbled.

We all knew that people were supposed to live for a hundred some-odd years, without ever getting sick or seeing anything troubling. The world was supposed to be a gentle place. A safe place.

```
<list:dialogue>
     <d: A life span is fixed, immutable.>
     <d: Our world does not change.>
</list>
```

The illusion had just been smashed to pieces.

What would happen next?

Perhaps imprudently, I was wondering that too. Surely, the suicides hadn't been the end of it. This had to be part of somebody's plan—maybe even a still-alive Miach Mihie's plan. The ones who had committed suicide were simply the first sacrifices that had to be made so that the plan could be put into action.

"Aren't you scared?" I asked the Interpol agent.

"Of course I am," he answered calmly.

"What did you want to talk to me about?"

Vashlov shrugged and began. "It was, I think, about a year ago when my section of Interpol began investigating a certain group. The group consists of powerful elders in various admedistrations and the heads of certain medical industrial collectives, as well as a few scholars and scientists. They were researching ways to improperly access people's WatchMe and medcare units in order to activate a certain technology during crises."

"What kind of technology?"

"We're not entirely sure yet. All we know is that they are able to use the admedistration WatchMe servers to access people's bodies directly. That, and their ideology reflects strong memories of the Maelstrom."

The Maelstrom—the years of chaos and mushroom clouds that had opened mankind's eyes to its true nature and inspired our current lifeist society.

"They—these old people—are afraid that humanity will once again fall into the chaos of those years. There are plenty of theories as to why the Maelstrom happened, but one thing it did prove was that our brains are capable of reverting to barbarism with shocking alacrity. And it only took tens of millions of people to die to prove it. Which is why they moved to put all of humanity under observation—through WatchMe. They call themselves the Next-Gen Human Behavior Monitoring Group."

I had to collect my thoughts for a moment to process this story of megalomaniacal conspiracy. The man had Interpol ID, and he didn't seem delusional—it was just that the scale of his conspiracy theory was so grand. He was asking me to believe that all human life was basically under the watchful eye of a select group of people.

"There's no need to give me that look. I'll show you my Interpol psych evaluation, if you like."

"I'm just not sure how to take this." Of all the things I had anticipated this man telling me, a conspiracy theory was not one of them.

"I completely understand, but you're going to have to believe me. We do not have much time left."

"You mean there's going to be another wave of suicides?"

"Or something like that, yes. On the day of the incident, this group performed a test of their system. Just a test, to see if the technology worked as intended. The test was a success—save for an unexpected mass wave of simultaneous suicides."

"You mean to tell me that was an accident?"

I found it hard to believe that an organization founded on fear of the Maelstrom, no matter how megalomaniacal, would make a technology capable of ending so many lives and causing so much fear. Wasn't that exactly what they would be trying to prevent?

"No, not an accident. According to our source, there is another group within this group. Though they share the same objectives, they are directly opposed to the larger group on the issue of the means to that end. A rogue faction, if you will."

"So this ideological rift within the group was the trigger that caused all those deaths?"

"Rather, what we saw was one act in the confrontation between these two groups. The suicides were a power play by the rogue faction, if you will."

A little office spat among a group of megalomaniacs, resulting in a mountain of corpses.

"Then why bring this to me?" I asked.

"In order to ask for your help, of course. Rather, we want to help you with your investigation. I'll be frank. There are elements within Interpol that have not taken kindly to the Helix Inspection Agency inserting themselves into the investigation of the incident. There was quite a heated debate about it. The naysayers felt that this was strictly a criminal case, and that WHO, an admedistration monitoring agency, was using the incident as an excuse to make a grab for more authority."

"They were probably right."

Stauffenberg was first and foremost among the expansionists. I had once listened to her give a speech in which she claimed that the Helix Inspection Agency, as defenders of lifeism, had an obligation to deal with any and every threat to human lives or health.

"Even still, with what's happened, and worse to come, cooperation seems to be the only choice. We do not know when they will make the next move. All we know is that we have to stop them before—excuse me."

Vashlov put a hand to one ear. Someone calling him on his HeadPhone.

<horror>

Unconsciously, I reached up and rubbed the back of my own scalp.

Right inside here.

Inside the gray matter in my skull.

Some old farts, in their fear of the Maelstrom, had built a little medicule network there for me. Our free will was the last thread of ourselves not yet outsourced. Yet there was a mechanism that could take even that away from me, a mechanism controlled by a group of people that didn't believe in our society, not that they wanted us to believe in it. If that network suddenly ordered me to kill myself, then I would draw the gun I wore at my side and, without a single conflicting thought, shoot myself in the head. I found myself really wanting to know exactly how it would work when the time came.

```
</horror>
```

This was the result of outsourcing all our bodily functions. By entrusting our bodies to others through WatchMe, we had reached the point where we could no longer support our own selves without those external mechanisms to help us.

Humans are good at dividing up labor.

```
<list:protocol>
    <p: Hunt pig.>
    <p: Cut up pig.>
    <p: Cook pig.>
</list>
```

Food must've been a very personal thing for most people in the beginning. Now, the whole process had been divided into so many stages, each with their own specialists. I doubted anyone today really understood the routes food took from its origins to their mouths.

Vashlov tapped me on the shoulder. "Got a news report coming in on Network 24. Check it out."

I called up a media channel in one corner of my field of vision. I linked to Network 24 and immediately saw the EMERGENCY NEWS REPORT tag. A newscaster with a nervous look on his face began reading from the prompter on his AR.

"Good day, this is Edison Carter. What we are about to broadcast is the contents of a memorycel we received at our news bureau just moments ago. The memorycel contains a message from a person claiming responsibility for the recent mass suicide incident."

"What's this all about?" I asked Vashlov.

He shook his head in disbelief. "I wish I knew. We'll just have to watch."

The self-review committee at Network 24 had a reputation for being a little looser than other media outlets. A short while earlier, the image of a dead soldier appearing in a corner of one frame during a report on the violence in Chechnya had sparked an outcry against the station. Most other media outlets subjected everything they showed to an AI editor before broadcast in order to prevent any possibility of showing something emotionally traumatic. Relatively speaking, then, Network 24 was pretty extreme and as such not entirely worthless as a news source.

"We will begin playback now," Edison Carter said. The screen went black.

```
<log:media=Network24:id=225-78495hu6ryti5h23j-09>
```
I'm not sure when they'll play this, so let me wish you a good morning, a good day, and a good evening.
```
</log>
```

It was a female voice, heavily modulated.

There was no picture. Only the words VOICE ONLY in the middle of the screen.

I closed my eyes. Maybe that way I could hear a kernel of the real person—which could very well have been Miach Mihie. Besides, if there were no picture, what was the point of looking at it?

```
<log:media=Network24:id=225-78495hu6r-yti5h23j-09>
```
A lot of people have died.

A lot of people ended their own lives all at the same time.

I'm sure it was shocking.

I'm sure you're frightened at the possibility of seeing someone die before your eyes.

We did this.

Our methods are, at present, a secret.

However, the framework for the method is already inside
you, inside each of your brains.

It's too late to take it out now.

You are all our hostages.

</log>

I tried to listen through the warbling blips of whatever masking
process had been applied to the voice for a trace of Miach Mihie
and was unsuccessful.

<log:media=Network24:id=225-78495hu6r-yti5h23j-09>

You already know what we are capable of.

You're frightened. You're angry. You are experiencing
many emotions.

These emotions are real. Treasure them.

Our society has been engineered to suppress your
emotions.

You are being crushed beneath words of kindness.

This is not written anywhere. It is not the law.

Yet it binds you all the same. Never has there been a
generation so self-regulated. Never has there been a civiliza-
tion so weighted down by rules not generated from within,
but without.

No one can say what's really on their mind. Since we
were children, we have been told that we are vital resources
to our society. Our bodies do not belong to us, they belong
to society at large. They are public property.

Haven't you had enough of it?

I am sure you have all heard about the rise in the suicide
rate. You're not the only one who wants to escape.

</log>

The message was a familiar one.

Miach's words to me and Cian echoed in my head.

Words that had given a clear shape to our suffering.

<log:media=Network24:id=225-78495hu6r-yti5h23j-09>
We are going to create a new world.

In order to do that, we need to know who is capable of making change.

Within the next week, I want you each to kill at least one other person.

I don't care what means you have to use.

I want you to prove that you're capable of doing anything to serve your own ends. Prove that other people don't matter.

Accept the fact that your life is the most important. Revel in it.

Those who are unable or unwilling to perform this small task will die.

You know we can follow through with this threat. You have seen what we can do.

If you should hesitate to take someone else's life, even if it means saving yourself, then we will kill you without mercy.

That is, you will kill yourself.

We can do this with the press of a button.

For those who do not yet believe us, we will show you proof.

You will be able to see it for only a moment.

Watch closely.
</log>

"That is all the voice data we have received at Network 24." The screen switched back to Edison Carter. He was reading from an AR script again. "We traced the origin of the message, however. The person or people who sent it used the ID of one of the recent mass suicide victims." At that point, the star reporter of Network 24 casually reached into his shirt pocket, pulled out a pen, and slammed it into his right eye.

Vashlov covered his eyes.

The AI censor kicked in.

Before Carter began scrambling his own brains on a global feed, the image cut out, replaced by scrolling text apologizing for the emotionally traumatic visuals, and urging all viewers to seek appropriate therapy as soon as possible. They even displayed the ID of the nearest therapeutic center. Like therapy would negate the fact that Carter had just committed suicide in front of the world.

"Shit, I can't believe I just saw that. Shit!"

Vashlov was muttering under his breath.

On the battlefield, I had seen bodies with their heads blown off, abandoned corpses in advanced states of decay. As such, the image wasn't a particularly shocking one, but the circumstances were more than enough to give me pause.

If this really was Miach's doing, the girl needed serious therapy. She needed enough pharmaceuticals and counseling to rewire her brain.

I raced the car on to the airport. There was no time to waste. I had to get to Baghdad before the monster lurking beneath the heavy clouds of kindness awoke and bared its fangs.

02

<recollection>

I don't belong in this world.

The first time I had that thought was during an admedistration morality session. I was still in middle school, so I went as an observer with my parents. I say "went," but the session was in AR. The topics on the table began with some very nuanced, hard to define, and frankly meaningless points about the propriety of certain advertisements. Gradually though—I don't recall the particulars of how it happened now—the discussion shifted to moral concerns about the use of caffeine.

I had always thought that tea was tea.

Coffee was coffee.

Except that, just like all wine contained alcohol, these beverages contained caffeine.

`<antipathy>`

To this day I remember her clearly, the woman with a big voice who was running the show. I don't remember her name. She began very demurely, waiting for her turn to take the floor. Yet when she spoke, her words were anything but demure.

"I was just wondering if there isn't a moral problem with the taking of caffeine."

According to her, caffeine was basically

```
<list:item>
    <i: a stimulant.>
    <i: an excitement enhancer.>
    <i: bad for the stomach.>
    <i: an unhealthy substance.>
</list>
```

"Caffeine is essentially addictive," the woman said.

Very softly.

A gentle denunciation.

"It just seems to me," she went on to say, "that there is something *indecent* about the effects of long-term use."

`</antipathy>`

"What about those who require the use of caffeine in their occupation?" asked my father, the scientist. This was why I was soon to witness my father being verbally pummeled in public. Which was odd, because as far as I could tell, what he had said was correct, common sense, and altogether noninflammatory.

But the woman's argument was so in line with admedistration ideas of propriety, so modestly put—and so one-sided, so easy to understand, and so filled with determination.

Determination after determination.

People in the admedistrations liked other people to decide things for them. People who made decisions created an atmosphere. Scientists had always been bad at this. That was because the facts could be dry and were often complex; yet by necessity the truth must be plain enough to withstand repeated inquiry, all of which made it unappealing. So my father told me some time after the session had ended.

My father had said that certain occupations required the use of caffeine, and that there were certain kinds of stress that caffeine helped reduce.

<antipathy>

"The arguments Mr. Kirie gives us," the woman said, close to the end of the session, "are quite like the rationales given by those who clung to their tobacco and alcohol habits, even when everyone around them had abandoned the foul things."

<list:item>

    <i: She indicated evidence that caffeine caused panic attacks.>
    <i: She indicated that caffeine contributed to insomnia.>
    <i: She even went so far as to indicate that caffeine could cause seizures in some people.>
    <i: She noted that caffeine could act as a trigger for headaches and amnesia.>

</list>

</antipathy>

Not once did my father manage to get the word *moderation* in edgewise. Though caffeine wasn't about to be wholly abolished, the atmosphere in the session clearly colored caffeine as a poisonous, indecent substance to be avoided.

<antipathy>

I felt sick through most of the session.

Not an upset stomach. More of a spiritual queasiness. Like my mind wanted to vomit. To me, the woman was a menace, and I couldn't understand why everyone in the session seemed to be nodding and swallowing the venomous words she spat out like candy.

"I know it's not very realistic, but I have a dream that someday," the woman said in closing, "someday caffeine will be entirely abolished."

</antipathy>

<regret>

I regretted having asked my parents to take me with them to the session.

I remembered seeing a media channel where they showed picture after picture of food items I had never seen before in my life. When I asked my father what it was, he said they called it the "Two Minutes' Hate."

"It's for us, mainly, the last generation who ate food with too much fat, too much cholesterol, too much salt—food that's bad for your health and not properly resource-aware. We were to watch that and think 'I can't eat that. People who eat those things aren't fit to be in our society. They lack resource awareness. They're harming their public body.' It's a form of self-suggestion."

The program had aired regularly ten years before. And now the kind of hatred against unhealthy food that started with the Two Minutes' Hate had born fruit in the form of opinions like the one we heard in the session that day—a call for everyone to join in a shared hatred of caffeine.

I was proud of my father. He had created WatchMe. He had changed the world. I didn't want to see him shamed like this. If this was the admedistration, if this was the world, then I didn't want to be there. This was long before I met Miach, but my feeling of discomfort that day was so severe that I remembered the morality session for a long time afterward. The discomfort followed me to school, and even when I played games at home. It was always there, gnawing at my stomach. I never wanted to go to a session again.

`</regret>`

The first person to notice my discomfort was a girl reading a book by the jungle gym in the park I passed by on my way home from school. She walked up to me and asked if I knew why the jungle gym bars warped the way they did.

`</recollection>`

≡

"This is BirdRider with an announcement for all passengers. This Northern Passengers 947 DR flight out of Tokyo will be landing in the Baghdad Medopolis in one hour."

The announcement telling me my arrival time came like a soft whisper in my ear. Very pleasant. Unpleasant things were abhorred in this world.

No disease, no unsettling tastes, no disturbing images. If, by some gross miscalculation, you did happen across any of these things, there were plenty of therapists waiting to help.

A world devoid of unpleasantness. I wondered how much further we had to go until we reached a world devoid of life. The land of the dead.

While the silky soft voice sounded next to my ear, I leaned forward in my seat and looked out the window at the six main wings of the PassengerBird. The wings rippled and changed form, as if they were actually flapping as they curled around invisible currents of air. Back when airplanes had been the main form of aerial transportation, travel hadn't been half as elegant.

That put me in mind of the jungle gym again. The words from Miach's lips.

Even at the beginning of the twenty-first century, jungle gyms were still made of metal. Not intelligent, not morphable. Not even soft.

```
<list:item>
    <i: Miach, still alive>
    <i: Miach, who didn't die>
    <i: Miach, who didn't leave us behind>
    <i: Miach, who might have killed Cian, and
    2,795 other people besides>
</list>
```

I thought by now I was my own woman, but here I was, chasing after Miach's shadow again. For most of my time in flight, I had been reading a paper about healthy society that Professor Saeki had recommended to me. It turned out that there were many things the Nazis had started. PA systems, for instance. Before digital delivery and direct feeds to HeadPhones became widespread, these electronic devices magnified one's voice in order to broadcast information to many people at the same time. The autobahn had been the grandfather of our modern expressway. Funny that it was only scholars who seemed to associate the Nazis with a healthy society.

```
<recollection>
    "Hitler's mother died of breast cancer, you know,"
    Professor Saeki said. "Her doctor was a Jew. That's what
    started Hitler's hatred of the Jewish people. In other words,
    the Holocaust was born from Hitler's mother's breast...I
    forget whether it was the right or the left."
</recollection>
```

I left my seat and walked up the steps from the passenger area to the café on the PassengerBird's upper deck lounge. Up here, it was like you were standing on the roof of the Bird. Blue sky stretched in every direction, and the sea of clouds below shone a brilliant white, thick with moisture. Perhaps with this in mind, the floor had been made of a supple white material that gave softly under pressure, visually blending with the clouds at its edges. The walls of the PassengerBird were made of an intelligent material that went transparent when you looked at it, giving its passengers a panoramic view. If it were not for the thin lines of the PassengerBird's frame, it would have seemed like you were floating in the sky.

Everything in the world is floating in the sky.

When there's no disease, when time has stopped.

People who take nicotine know nothing of politeness.

Nicotine makes your arteries shrink and your blood run thick.

Schopenhauer and Kant both despised smoking, Professor Saeki told me.

I rested my elbows on the bar counter and ordered a small enough portion of caffeine to not break any rules of etiquette. Though tobacco and alcohol had been thoroughly obliterated, I was glad that caffeine had somehow managed to hang on. Even so, there were a lot of people who frowned at you if you ordered a cup of coffee, signs of a slowly building wave of momentum against caffeine. It had gotten worse in the last decade.

I went to one corner of the café and found a seat—one of several red gelatinous mushrooms protruding from the white deck. The café was completely empty. There were hardly any passengers either. I asked one of the attendants whether this was typical of the flight, and he agreed that numbers were down today.

Because the world had changed.

People were staying in their homes, thinking. No longer could anyone say for sure they wouldn't be dying anytime soon. Especially not the people who had witnessed the newscaster killing himself.

```
<list:item>
    <i: Do I believe the declaration?>
    <i: Will I kill someone?>
    <i: Who should I kill?>
</list>
```

To each, his or her own level of internal conflict.

Distress, hesitation, resentment, raw emotion.

Should I not kill and die, or should I kill and live? That was the question.

I imagined darkness sweeping through the households of the world in a churning wave of bleak emotions. Most admedistrations had called immediate sessions to discuss the declaration, but hardly anyone had shown up. What was there to discuss?

Okay, everyone, I'd like to start today's session.

Should we really kill others so that we can survive?

Should we use knives or blunt instruments?

No one here has a gun, do they?

I had a hard time imagining it. Yet if they didn't deal with the matter head on, what was left but empty platitudes? Calm down, everyone is going to be okay—even when they knew they wouldn't be. This wasn't something you could discuss in public. This was a decision everyone had to make on their own. At this moment, everyone in the world was being tested.

Just thinking about it made me grit my teeth and start fiddling with my fingers. It was times like this you really needed some nicotine.

It had been several days now since I'd had a smoke, and I missed it. I couldn't eat to compensate either, or I'd get fat, which would draw unwanted attention. Being fat was even worse than having bad skin. Deviations from standard physique really stood out when everyone was listening so attentively to their health consultant's advice and following their perfectly designed lifestyle plans to the letter. The range of acceptable body types grew narrower every year.

Q: How long will this game go on?

A: We want to keep everyone playing until the body fat ratio of everyone in the world is plus or minus 1 percent of everyone else of their own gender. There are several ways to quit the game along the way, such as death, death, or our favorite, death.

Maybe the ones who had killed themselves just wanted out.

```
<recollection>
```
Heidrich and Himmler tried to eliminate obesity among the SS, Professor Saeki said. Himmler's dream was that one day, all Germans would be vegetarians.
```
</recollection>
```

Maybe everyone wanted out of the game, but the atmosphere of conformity that society generated was too hard to break free of, and eventually, they gave up trying to quit. I had stayed in, myself, but in ways that didn't require me to be serious about it at all. This meant that I had to spend most of my time on the fringes, tromping across battlefields.

```
<dictionary>
    <item>Baghdad</item>
<definition>
```
Capital city of Iraq. Located in the middle of Iraq on the Mesopotamian plain. Baghdad is an old city, built during the rule of the Abbasid Caliphate and nearly destroyed in a wave of terrorist attacks against a U.S. occupying force stationed there following the second Gulf War at the beginning of this century. After the Maelstrom, Baghdad reinvented itself as a medical industry mecca. Tax breaks favoring medical investors and laws allowing the testing of experimental treatments on humans made the city an attractive place for medical industrial combines, medical think

tanks, and research organizations, all who raced to establish their headquarters here, giving rise to the city's nickname, "Medical Dubai."

```
</definition>
</dictionary>
```

I looked through the passenger compartment and saw that, indeed, most people were somehow tied to the medical industry.

```
<list:item>
    <i: a researcher for a medical industrial
    collective>
    <i: a top economist for one of the medical
    think tanks>
    <i: a software engineer manager for a medcare
    unit maker>
</list>
```

Of course, when I thought about it, it was difficult to find someone in our modern society who didn't have a connection to some sort of medical service. I was reminded that my Helix agent ID made me stand out like a sore thumb. Especially with me standing up here, doing caffeine.

I scrunched down into my gelatin seat and watched as the PassengerBird wheeled through the sky. The seat twisted beneath me, absorbing the extra Gs as we descended to the Baghdad landing deck.

≡

It didn't take long for the first cracks to appear in the world's facade.

```
<movie:ar:id-593-6586afv50-73649o-arin678>
```

   While I was in the PassengerBird an Italian man hanged himself: Luigi Vercotti, a volunteer resource manager in the Weiland Admedistration.

   Vercotti had a six-year-old son and a thirty-eight-year-old wife. He had made a loop in a necktie while his wife and child were out shopping, tied it to a rafter, and kicked the small crate he'd been standing on out from under his feet.

   The weight of his entire body falls on his neck.

   The carotid artery begins to scream under the pressure.

   The brain ceases to function in less than ten seconds' time.

   Then, gradually, the heart. stops. beating.

```
</movie>
```

Inside his body, WatchMe was blaring with emergency messages for the medical server. Even when it was all over, the medicules would keep racing about until they ran out of energy from furiously signaling that there didn't seem to be enough oxygen getting to the brain. Seen from the outside, death was a very gradual process of cell decomposition. It took time. Death didn't happen in an instant.

Miach once showed me a picture scroll from the twelfth century or so called the "Nine Faces Poem."

It consisted of nine illustrations showing a woman who had died. Her body gradually changed color, became bloated, then began to rot. The scroll ended with various birds and animals coming to eat her. The pictures were real, raw. It was hard to imagine the thing had been drawn so long ago. I had no idea how Miach had gotten her hands on such obviously emotionally traumatic material. Though I assumed she was capable of pretty much anything that was illegal.

"At the time when this was written, death was everywhere," Miach said. "It takes time for a person to die, lots of time. When we go to someone's great-grandfather's or great-grandmother's funeral these days, they have that case for melting and sterilizing the body. But back then, they put the body in a coffin and put the whole thing in the ground. You've probably never even seen a coffin, have you?

"Even when they processed the bodies, they didn't take them to a reduction center to have them converted into harmless goop, they actually burned them. When they said 'dust to dust,' they really meant it."

The idea that human death comes with brain death is a pretty recent one. From the time when people started thinking that we were our brains.

The moment I stepped off the bird in Baghdad, a call came in from the local Helix Agency office. I opened the message in my call box and I was in a real-time AR feed. There were reports from the Italian police in a document list and feeds with chatter about an incident that had happened thirty minutes prior. More was coming in: evidence, witness statements, etc.

"Is this the work of our mastermind or masterminds?" Someone in AR asked. Stauffenberg was there. She shook her head and indicated to all of us that we should read the suicide note posted in evidence.

"He left a note?" someone else said, surprised. No one had left anything in the earlier wave of suicides, with the possible exception of Cian Reikado.

The suicide note was a simple affair.

```
<list:item>
    <i: I do not think I am capable of killing
    another person.>
    <i: I do not think I could bear the guilt I would
    feel even if I did manage to kill someone.>
    <i: Though my body is a public body, the same
    goes for others around me.>
    <i: I will not let myself be killed by the
    evil people who claim to be doing this.>
    <i: I apologize to my wife and son, and
```

```
    my neighbors, for choosing to kill myself
    instead.>
</list>
```

That was all.

"This is a new development. We do not think our mastermind was involved," Stauffenberg said.

I had to agree. This wasn't the doing of whoever had sent that memorycel to Network 24. This was someone who had taken that news report seriously and decided to take their own life before the "mastermind" could take it for him. It wasn't an entirely outrageous decision.

Stauffenberg asked about media coverage and was informed that at present the only people other than the family who knew about the suicide were the local Italian police, Interpol, and the Helix Inspection Agency. Still, they would probably only be able to keep it under wraps for a few days at most. After that, the Werther effect would sweep the globe.

That was why they were giving the media a gag order, to keep would-be Werthers from popping up. Incidentally, the Werther effect refers to multiple linked suicides after a widely publicized one. Why did I know this mostly useless fact? Because Miach Mihie had told me.

```
<recollection>
```
"See this?" Miach held up a book. "*The Sorrows of Young Werther*. This book killed a lot of people. Impressive, isn't it?"

How does a book kill people, I asked her. "You mean someone hit them with it?"

So Miach explained the travails of *jungen* Werther to me. Apparently, the titular character loves this girl, but the girl is engaged to marry another man. Unable to bear unrequited love, our hero kills himself.

"Sounds like a pretty typical romantic love tragedy,"

I said. "What does that have to do with lots of people dying?"

"Get this—people who identified with Werther, because, say, they were in a similar position, were influenced by the story to kill themselves. Then people heard about that and *they* killed themselves. The first copycat suicides! And all after a completely fictional character, though no doubt inspired by the author Goethe's own experiences."

Miach Mihie flashed her customary smile and thrust the book out in front of her. "Isn't it cool? Words, books, fiction all have the power to kill."

</recollection>

Useless information, rotting at the bottom of the world.

I knew these things, thanks to Miach.

If word of the suicide and the accompanying note got out, it was a sure thing that plenty of other people would follow suit. I wondered how many would choose suicide before we reached the time limit, and how many people would do as they were told and kill at least one other person. It occurred to me that there would be a lot of people unable to kill themselves or another person who would simply try to wait it out.

Either way, it was clear we were headed for another Maelstrom.

"Couldn't we take everyone's WatchMe off-line and cut the links to the health supervision servers?" someone suggested, but it was an impractical idea. WatchMe was tied into the global ID system. If a person took their WatchMe off-line, they couldn't buy things, get on the train, or even get into their own home. It would be mass chaos.

"The world will fall into chaos," grumbled one of the other Helix agents in the AR session. Then the weary-faced agents all began to talk at once, their words describing a grand list of what we would lose.

"All the admedistrative functions: hitch-homing, morality sessions, mutual aid, elder care. All will cease."

"Our social system is based on the open exchange of information and unlimited trust in others within the admedistration and regional collectives. What will happen to that?"

"And our economic cycle is based on the assumption that people will live long, healthy lives."

"Things will grind to a halt."

"What's to keep people from killing each other? From killing us?"

"If things keep going this way—"

"We'll be back to the beginning of the twenty-first century, no—"

"There will be no morality at all! Another Maelstrom!"

"They've activated some kind of process in the brain. The question is, what?"

"Clearly, what we've seen is the forced introduction of artifical *intent*. What I'd like to know is who is doing this?"

"According to Senior Inspector Tuan Kirie's report, there already exists a paper describing in detail the structures in the brain that express human will. The paper is a study by Russian neurologist Sergey Gorlukovich Yelensky on the feedback system of the midbrain." Prime was speaking. "This paper details how to very accurately model the human psyche control system and has already influenced some practicing therapists. I believe our agent has some solid evidence related to this paper that will help us get to the core of our current dilemma."

"Unfortunately, that's not true," I said. "I'm merely in a position to contact someone who I believe *may* have the kind of information that will lead us back to those responsible."

"Well, whatever the case, the fact that you're ahead of us in this investigation remains unchanged."

One of the other agents spoke up. "If they understand that much about human will, it's possible they can in fact control it. Senior Inspector Kirie, shouldn't you share any information you have with the rest of us?"

He spoke very gently. This was a discussion. No feathers were to be ruffled.

This was how it was done.

"At the present moment I have no solid information. The scraps I do have on hand would only needlessly confuse the investigation as a whole. I did not see the need to contact any other members of this agency."

"I think that I should be the judge of what is solid and what is not," Stauffenberg said, narrowing her eyes.

I gave a noncommittal nod and imagined how good it would feel to just give her the finger.

```
<recollection>
```
    "That's a symbol? What does it mean?" I asked, looking at Miach's raised middle finger.

    "It's an ancient gesture. It means *fuck you*. That's English, though the phrase isn't even in use anymore, so it's kind of hard to feel the impact it once had. Imagine all the worst things you could possibly say to someone to show how little you think of them. That's *fuck you*."
```
</recollection>
```

03

Gabrielle Étaín says: "We are a collection of desires, defined along a hyperbolic curve."

Gabrielle Étaín says: "Even the pigeon and the monkey overestimate the value of that which is in front of them."

Gabrielle Étaín says: "Even the pigeon and the monkey have a consciousness and a will. What makes our consciousnesses and our wills any more important?"

I was in my car, driving to meet Gabrielle Étaín.

The Tigris spread out to my right-hand side as I passed beneath an arch, massive and white like the rib bone of a dragon. The road sloped up toward the top level of the giant Dian Cécht medical industrial collective building that loomed like an ant

mound over Baghdad, gradually giving me a better view of the
landscape as I got closer. Eventually, I was high enough to look
down on all of Baghdad. I sat back and let the Baghdad Central
Traffic Guidance server lead me to Gabrielle Étaín's lab.

The desert horizon shimmered in the heat.

The medical industrial collective zone in Baghdad lacked any
of the advertising you saw in regular cities. In other words, the
medical complex here was entirely self-sufficient. There was no
need to sell AR advertising space. Looking at it, you could see how
no one here needed the extra revenue. Still, for someone who had
grown up with advertisements plastered on every visible surface,
being in a place with none was somewhat disconcerting.

I saw a forest of pinkish evergreens and a lake. That would
be the Dian Cécht park sector. I drove around the "naturally"
modeled shore within the giant complex. The design group
responsible for building the place had taken care to *not* make it
feel like an anthill once you were inside the thing. The car took
me up a gently curving slope to the floor above the lake. This
was the uppermost level in the entire zone.

I stopped the car. The SEC Neuromedical Research Consortium
offices thrust out like the bow of a boat, six hundred twenty
meters up the side of the Dian Cécht. That would be the research
and development sector, sitting out under the blazing sun. SEC
was an acronym formed from the first letters of its founding
admedistrations: Sukunabikona, Eugene, Crups.

I touched the door to give my ID and a receptionist came out
to show me into the waiting room. The interior here reminded
me of the PassengerBird: high ceilings and walls made of a white,
plastic-like material, with red gelatin seats here and there, all
unoccupied.

I sat down in one and waited until Gabrielle Étaín made
her appearance. I heard her shoes squeak on the floor before I
looked up. We shook hands, and she sat down with me on one
of the red seats.

"When I heard a Helix agent was here to see me I thought

it was a surprise inspection. Not that we are doing any research here to concern anyone at the WHO."

She spoke softly and slowly, sitting with her back to a window that stretched the full length of the wall. The horizon behind her formed a straight line dividing sky from water. Several birds wheeled through the air.

"I'm sorry if I startled you. It was unintentional. I'm here to ask after a particular person and about certain neurological research. I have reason to believe you can help me on both points."

"By all means."

"First, the research. Are you familiar with a paper that lays out, in great detail, the feedback mechanisms in the midbrain?"

"Yelensky's paper?"

"That's the one," I said, watching her face closely.

She moved her lips like she was rolling a candy around in her mouth, staring at me a moment before she said, "This *is* an inspection, then."

I waved both hands in denial. "No, it's not, really. All I'm asking for is information that we think can help with an ongoing investigation. Why do you think this is an inspection?"

"Because our neuromedical consortium is putting together a model of those very mechanisms you speak of."

"Then, do you think you could explain the general gist of your research to me—just whatever's been publicly announced. I don't mean to pry," I said as gently as I could.

Étaín thought for several seconds before telling me that the consortium was researching the nature of value judgments within the human psyche.

"What sort of judgments?" I asked.

"Say, for instance, if I offered someone ten thousand credits now or a promise for twenty thousand credits a year from now, which would they choose?"

"The former, probably."

"Indeed. And this is true not only of humans but also of primates such as chimpanzees, and birds such as pigeons and pheasants. Similar desire tendencies can be observed in other animals typically kept as pets, such as dogs and cats. This category of organisms overestimates the value of that which is right in front of it."

"Is that something we evolved?"

"It's part of our genetic programming. However, to find the same feature across so many varied species indicates that there is some reason this is a particularly easy feature for vertebrates to develop."

"Well, isn't it kind of obvious? If we don't eat the thing sitting right in front of us, some other individual will come along and take it away. Individuals who sit around waiting for a future reward would die in such a world. Isn't valuing the bird in hand just part of the survival of the fittest?"

"If you plot perceived value on a graph, with the horizontal axis as time and the present as zero, then you will see the line representing value curve sharply upward the closer it comes to the zero point, reaching its zenith as it hits the vertical axis. By comparison, value in the far future goes low quickly, changing hardly at all between a year and two years distant. A hyperbola. When humans and most living creatures consider the value of something, they tend to see its future value diminish hyperbolically."

"In other words, our system of evaluation isn't exponentially logical, it's hyperbolically illogical."

"Indeed. And because we possess a hyperbolic value system, we make illogical decisions and take precipitate actions. When a chance to profit presents itself clearly before our eyes, we erroneously believe its value to be much greater than it actually is. There is an ongoing survival game between the agents of short-term desire and long-term desire, and we call this game *will*. This is an important feature of the feedback mechanism that Yelensky's model of human will does not consider—a model we are currently using our findings to perfect."

I thought of my father. If you wanted to use the feedback

mechanism to control human will, you would need a very detailed model of human value judgments in order to accurately predict how such control would function.

"Dr. Nuada Kirie wouldn't be part of the project team, would he?"

"He is, that is, he was in the beginning. He is no longer with the consortium."

"Was Dr. Kirie using this midbrain feedback web model for any other research?"

"Well…some of our researchers do take part in side projects, but I'm afraid I wouldn't know about any of that."

"How does knowing that the feedback web follows a hyperbolic curve change your view of human will compared to previous models?" I asked out of plain curiosity.

Étaín put a hand to her chin in thought for a moment. "Well, I suppose the revelation that human will is actually more of a battle royal between multiple desire agents within the brain has allowed us to prove that animals too possess a will."

"In other words, animals aren't just acting by their genetic programming or instinct?"

"Your language reveals a bias. What we call our 'will' or 'soul' is really just a collision between multiple genetically programmed elements. There is a test using pigeons where one button releases ten beans when it's pressed and thirty beans when it's pressed after waiting a certain amount of time. It turns out that there are pigeons who choose to wait for the thirty beans. Pigeons have the same range of choice allowed them by will under our model. In other words, the model allows us not only to understand human will but the very nature of consciousness, and put that knowledge to better use."

"Such as?"

"Such as…pain," she said.

"Excuse me?"

"First, you have to understand the true nature of what I have been referring to as feedback. Any psychological effect that grabs the attention of the consciousness and leaves a strong impression is feedback. This is true under Yelensky's model as well. The feedback need not be a reward or even anything beneficial."

"All right. And?"

"The pain we feel the moment we prick our finger with a needle is nothing more than another agent trying to leave an impression and get selected. The hyperbolic time axis in this case is very short, making it easier for the pain to be chosen."

I frowned. How could pain be chosen? "But you can't accept or deny pain," I said.

"Actually, you can. Surely you have heard stories of people who are so focused on some activity that they only realize their finger or arm has been cut off some seconds after the fact. This is because the pain competed with, yet failed to overcome, the hold that activity had on their consciousness."

"I see."

"That is why we understand pain to be a subjective experience. For a physical sensation, it is highly dependent on environmental factors to determine whether or not it is selected and to what degree. That is why there is no absolute scale to measure pain."

"So all of the sensations that make up our reality are these agents who have been selected for advancement to the upper levels of the brain?"

"That's one way to put it, yes. Even sight, sound, smell, and taste must be selected before they are permitted into the consciousness," Étaín said. "Of course, these basic stimuli have steep hyperbolas, making it easy for them to make the final cut, so they are rarely entirely ignored."

"Which means that, in a sense, your research isn't just about our consciousness, but about how our very reality is constructed."

Étaín raised an eyebrow and looked at me as though I had said something peculiar. "But reality and consciousness are the same thing, Inspector Kirie."

"Are they?"

"The reality we can accept is limited to our consciousness, after all."

"I suppose you're right."

Gabrielle Étaín stood and extended her hand. "I hope I have answered all of your questions to your satisfaction, Inspector Kirie. Now, if you don't mind, I should get back to my work."

I thanked her and shook her hand, saying that I might be back again. Just then, I became suddenly curious as to how this woman had taken the news of the declaration. I wondered what decision she would make.

I loved asking the uncomfortable questions.

"By the way, I was wondering whether you heard the declaration."

"I did."

"What did you think?"

It wasn't a fair question. But I was hoping that its very vagueness might catch her by surprise and reveal something. Her response was disappointing.

"It's quite horrible."

I pressed the attack. "Don't you think the technology you're researching here treads similar ground to the mind-control suicides they threatened?"

Étaín's finger went to her chin again. "I'd have to agree. But we are not criminals. We cannot control another's will nor show them a different reality."

"Have plans to do anything before the deadline?"

Uncomfortable question number two.

Étaín furrowed her brow at my lack of tact. "I will do nothing. It's clear they're just trying to scare us."

"But they might actually have the technology to make people kill themselves. You saw what that newscaster did."

"And I trust the various admedistration members will show us their public resolve. Our society will bow to no one."

It was a pitch-perfect response. Perhaps too perfect.

Étaín showed me to the door in silence. As I walked through, a final question occurred to me. The drama of the moment was a bit forced, but sometimes that could be quite effective.

"One last thing, you don't happen to know of any organization called the Next-Gen Human Behavior Monitoring Group, do you?"

There was a brief moment of silence before Étaín's calm reply.

"Never heard of them."

04

The media was showing video of armed troops stationed in every major city in the world.

Streets lined with pink trees.

Pink paint to camouflage the rough edges of the city for its citizens.

Pink firearms.

Pink grenades.

Pink gas masks.

I had no doubt that the tear gas would be pink too.

The admedistrations had demanded every region in the world declare a state of emergency.

```
<list:item>
     <i: New York>
     <i: Paris>
     <i: Geneva>
     <i: Tokyo>
</list>
```

Police and Geneva Convention forces stood at every corner.

Their orders were to watch for killers and potential suicides. The killers would probably be wearing pink. Of course, since the police officers and soldiers on patrol were all subject to the same one-man-one-kill declaration, who could trust them? Everyone was suspect, and armed people even more so.

From the moment of the declaration, the world had been walking backward through history. People saw the Maelstrom in every shadow.

The central district of Baghdad was completely abandoned. Everyone was huddled in their homes as if they could avoid having to make a decision. But the declaration had made its effectiveness clear, and everyone belonging to an admedistration who had WatchMe installed was at risk.

It was hard when you were forced to make a very personal decision in a society that stressed following advice and cooperative consensus.

```
<list:item>
    <i: Should I kill someone to live?>
    <i: Should I kill no one and die?>
    <i: Should I choose not to believe what I saw
    with my own eyes?>
</list>
```

I had no doubt that the tech-heads were busily combing the admedistration servers, looking for holes in security. Holes in the WatchMe servers responsible for monitoring the medicules in several billion people's bodies.

For my part, I had just used my privileges as a Helix agent to slip some eavesdropping medicules into Gabrielle Étaín when I shook her hand. The medicules went in through the skin, finding their way through her body, until they activated the eavesdropping circuit in her HeadPhone. Though there hadn't been a single thing wrong with Étaín's performance to make me suspect her, she was the only lead I had.

A call came in from business-card man as I drove down the deserted road.

"Did you meet with Gabrielle Étaín?" Vashlov asked. He

sounded pleased with himself.

"Word travels fast."

"The SEC Neuromedical Research Consortium is just one public front of the Next-Gen Human Behavior Monitoring Group. Étaín is one of them, Inspector Kirie."

"And you know this how?"

"We followed the money. I realize that's a bit beyond the capabilities of a Helix agent."

"Then why not bug Gabrielle Étaín instead of me?"

"Oh, we are. With little result. She knows she's being watched."

"Then why didn't you stop me from going to see her? If I'd known she was involved—"

"Because we were hoping for a chemical reaction."

\<discomfort\>

> *That* was troubling. So the man from Interpol had used me, letting me meet with Étaín in hopes that the specter of an official agency investigation would elicit a reaction from the Next-Gen group. They had reached a dead end with their informants and surveillance, so they put their money on my being just the element of surprise they needed to tip the scales.
>
> "Well, don't I feel stupid."
>
> "You understand how critical the situation is. They might take defensive action. Take care of yourself."
>
> "Oh, I always do. There's no shortage of terrorists who would like a Helix agent as a feather in their cap."

\</discomfort\>

I ended the call to my HeadPhone and pulled in to the Baghdad Hotel.

Back when this had been a war zone, the American occupying forces had surrounded the place with four concrete walls to keep out the improvised explosive devices and the RPGs. In the middle of the explosions and the debris, the CIA had set up camp here. Though most surveillance of the terrorist sector these days was carried out by Geneva Convention forces and the military information suppliers they hired, at the time, the CIA was the largest information network run by any nation in the world.

That age had passed, and now the place was just a typical upscale hotel on Sadoon Street, where it passed through the Baghdad Medical Industrial Zone. Coming from Geneva forces camps on the front lines, I preferred less ostentatious places to stay, but there was a tradition of WHO and admedistration officials coming to the Baghdad Hotel, so I had little choice in the matter. I went through the lobby, passing by admedistration officers and WHO VIPs along the way. When I reached my room and pressed my finger to the door, it swung open. A single folded piece of paper fell to the floor.

<cautiously>

Reflexively, I switched off my AR. I didn't want anyone who might be snooping on my visual feed to see what, if anything, was written on the note. Like I had been able to see those records of the suicidees, the police and Interpol and certain civilian MIS had the authority to snoop on visual feeds in real time. Just to be sure, I went into the bathroom and used removal liquid to wash the AR contacts out of my eyes. Then I shut the door and crawled under the bed. Interpol was using me. They could easily be monitoring my room. Curled up like a fetus in the dark, I opened the twice-folded paper.

ABŪ-NUWĀS. EVENING. NO AR, NO RIDERS.

I crawled out from beneath the bed and looked out the window.

The sky was slowly growing redder, getting ready for dusk. By riders they meant visual and audio bugs. Someone wanted me to see or hear something they didn't want

recorded by AR and sent to any servers.
```
</cautiously>
```

Evening was pretty soon.

In a movie Miach showed me once, someone who'd received a secret message had used a lighter to burn it in an ashtray. How convenient that must've been, I thought as I changed into my civilian clothes and shoved the paper into a pocket.

It was very rare to see an actual Iraqi within the area occupied by the medical industrial collective. It had been a strange chain of events that led to this Middle Eastern country becoming the world center for medicine. But like there was no place better than any other for making movies or manufacturing PassengerBirds, there was no best place for making medicine. Once a little bit of wealth had accumulated, it had taken off, transforming the desert into a giant industrial zone.

The fact that Iraq had, during the Maelstrom, suffered from nuclear fallout meant that there was no shortage of disease here for medical researchers to study. But in those days, it would have been hard to find a place that *hadn't* been hit by nukes. Nor were the tax breaks and morally lax laws enough to explain the bizarre medical oasis that had sprung into existence here. The only explanation you could give was teleological: the wealth had accumulated here because of an accumulation of wealth.

Military resource suppliers took care of the security.

```
<list:company>
    <c: Security Arts Co.>
    <c: Hard Shield Co.>
    <c: Eugene & Crups Co.>
    <c: etc., etc.>
</list>
```

The zone was completely reliant on military resource supplier security.

Though from the nineteenth century to the twentieth century nonstanding forces had still been the property of nations, as the nations weakened, the balance of military force shifted to MRSs and military information suppliers. On the surface, there was very little difference, though, seeing as how nearly all MRSs and military information suppliers were contracted by the Geneva Convention Organization, an international body formed by an accord between every admedistration. I stopped at a SecGate in the several kilometer–long wall surrounding the medical zone so a medical soldier in his pink uniform could check my identification. They also needed my acknowledgment that they could not guarantee my well-being outside the security zone, and that my WatchMe would go off-line.

I was free, once again in a world without WatchMe, medcare units, or AR. I looked around at scenery that time had forgotten: barracks after barracks after barracks, a tangle of crumbling buildings. The place had a feel to it that was completely missing from any admedistration city, and the air was filled with scents and smells.

A man sat on the street smoking tobacco out of a giant pipe that looked more like a strange musical instrument. There was the smell of fish cooking, meats, and all kinds of spices. This was a market. I went into a nearby restaurant and ordered a meal of uncertain composition, calories, and risk vectors. I noticed an ashtray on the table, so I motioned to the owner that I wanted to smoke. He produced some cigarettes and a lighter. I took the memo I had stuck in my pocket, held it over the ashtray, and set it on fire. Cool. I'd always wanted to do that.

<relax>

This was life outside the admedistration. This was living.

It pleased me that even with the world medical headquarters looming over them, most people in lower Baghdad hadn't installed WatchMe. They weren't connected to any server. They just

```
<list>
    <i: caught colds.>
    <i: got headaches.>
    <i: got cancer.>
    <i: died around the age of sixty or seventy.>
</list>
```

I puffed on the cigarette, my first since Niger. Living here wouldn't be so bad, though I had my doubts as to how long the admedistrations would leave these people to their own devices.

Pretty soon my fish came out. It looked like a carp that had been caught in the nearby Tigris, sliced open and grilled. It came with a ball of some kind of bread and uncooked dates.

```
<list>
    <i: no calorie count>
    <i: no list of ingredients>
    <i: no risk assessment>
</list>
```

My simple dish, with no AR readout floating over it, was beautiful in its simplicity.

"That looks great," I said under my breath. Uncooked dates had been a rare delicacy for the desert people here, and maybe still were. Thus dates' status as symbols of beauty and victory in the Bible. I had heard that the Tree of Life in the Christian tradition was sometimes thought to have been a date palm. When he came into Jerusalem, the people of the city had waved date fronds to bless Jesus. This fruit was life, and faith.

I knew this not because Miach had ever told me, but because of the date palm pictured in the symbol of the Helix Inspection Agency. Any Christian overtones in that were nullified by the fact that the date palm had appeared as a symbol of life in the Koran and even in the tale of Gilgamesh—another local favorite in its day.

There were lots of people out in the street, the polar opposite of the state of affairs in the post-declaration admedistrative society I'd just left. I doubted many of the folks here had even heard the news. Only the billions of people with WatchMe installed had reason to be scared shitless. The residents of the lifeist block, responsible for 80 percent of the global economy. For the Iraqis on this twilight street, WatchMe and medicules had nothing to do with their lives.

Life on the outside, life on the inside.

The difference between the two couldn't be greater.

On one side, people cut up their bodies and entrusted the parts to different service providers in order to fulfill the functions demanded of them by society. On the other, these people weren't letting anyone touch their bodies.

As I busied myself with the river fish—the dish was called *masgouf,* I learned—the proprietor brought a bowl of watery yogurt. This I decided was less a dessert and more another course in the meal. He set it down on the pitted surface of my wooden table and retreated into the back.

</relax>

As he left, I noticed another piece of paper sticking out from beneath the yogurt bowl. I opened it. It said "To the river" in Japanese.

I motioned for the lighter again and burned the second piece of paper over my ashtray. Finished with the *masgouf,* I went out onto the street, weaving my way through the crowd in hopes of losing the tail my mystery correspondent doubtlessly feared.

This street had once been an entertainment district: Abū-Nuwās.

The name referred to this street, the one with the market. Abū-Nuwās had been a great Arab poet and a lover of wine and carnal pleasures in an Islamic society that forbade alcohol. His hedonistic poems took the list of things forbidden by Islam and threw it out the window—social shock poetry. In other words, two thousand years ago, a man had lived here who fought against the same kind of dogma that lifeist society espoused today. It was the perfect setting for a secret rendezvous between a spineless conformist to the system and someone who very likely had a hand in controlling the system.

I made a careful scan for tails, then left Abū-Nuwās for the banks of the river, glowing in the evening sun. The riverbank was open sand all the way down to the water. I wondered if it would be Gabrielle Étaín waiting for me, or even Miach Mihie herself. The light reflected off the Tigris, playing tricks with the eyes and hiding the face of the person I now saw standing a short distance away from me, closer to the river.

"You know why they call this place Mesopotamia?" the figure on the bank asked in a familiar voice. "*Mesopotamia* means 'between the rivers.' You understand?"

"Because we're between the Tigris and Euphrates?"

"Precisely."

The man stepped closer. He was wearing a tattered suit. A hobo suit. Fitting for the man who had left my mother and me thirteen years ago to come to Baghdad.

05

"I'm surprised you came all this way."

It was my father. The genuine article. Though his face bore the wear and tear of thirty years, it was still the same face as the man who had been defeated in that session by the caffeine-hating woman, and the man who had left me and my mother after Miach died.

It hadn't been easy getting here.

A lot of people died.

I told him that.

"I've heard. The whole world has it pretty bad right now. It's a shame."

"A shame? But didn't you tell Miach to kill them?"

"Not true," my father said, his back to the setting Baghdad sun.

"Have you been here this whole time? Thirteen years?"

He shook his head slowly. "I left on occasion. With an ID from my current organization I can go most places in the world without revealing who I am."

"Organization? Which organization might that be?"

"The only organization truly capable of controlling the world—the Next-Gen Human Behavior Monitoring Group. All the resources and medical planning take place here in the Dian Cécht complex."

"What exactly do you mean by control the world?"

My father began to walk slowly down the riverbank. I walked alongside him, listening carefully to every word.

"You've heard something from Saeki, yes? Or Étaín?"

"I've learned that human will is the state of struggle between various agents in a feedback web located in the midbrain. And I've learned that the hyperbola traced by that feedback influences our decisions."

"That's basically true, yes."

The sun had set and the temperature began dropping. It made the midday heat seem like a dream. I rubbed my hands together against the slight chill, glad I had thought to wear a jacket.

"And you're doing research into this?"

"No. The research is pretty much completed."

I hesitated. If the research were completed, then what was the Next-Gen group doing now? What was my father working on?

"Our organization's goal is to be prepared. We prepare for the possible coming collapse. We keep our technology safe, secret, and ready to deploy should the need ever arise. Of course, we would prefer that time never come, but Miach's group sees things somewhat differently."

"Explain."

"Hmm. Well, you seem to have already grasped the workings of the feedback mechanism and how it generates what we call *will*."

"Professor Saeki said it was like a conference."

"An analogy we often use. One important thing to understand, however, is the reflexive nature of the system. Based on the outcome of this 'conference,' the feedback mechanism is exposed to endless change and adjustment. The results influence our feedback system, and the feedback system generates more results in a loop. If we make a decision, that bias will increase in a cyclical fashion. The chaos in the system multiplies. This is why human will is illogical, never static, and very hard to predict. You follow?"

"I think so."

"In controlling the feedback web in the midbrain with medicules, we found we were able to influence human decisions, emotions, and thoughts. This all happened shortly before you were born. At that time, the control of human will was a hot topic with upper leadership at WHO and some of the admedistrations."

That would be the frightened old men.

Frightened of chaos.

Frightened of people losing their rational minds.

Frightened of riots leading to genocide leading to nukes going off all over our planet.

"The Maelstrom," I said, half to myself.

My father nodded. "At the time, the idea was to create a safety net to prevent mankind from ever sliding back into the disorder of those days. They called on us to do something about it. They thought we could find a way to save us from our own barbarous selves. Thus the Next-Gen Human Behavior Monitoring Group was born."

The group was no mere research organization, my father explained. In a way, it had more power than the United Nations, more power even than WHO. These powerful, frightened old men and women who were part of WHO and the United Nations and the admedistrations were also part of the Next-Gen group.

"We had all the funding we needed, and research progressed swiftly. It wasn't long before we had medicules in past the blood-brain barrier," he said.

"What?"

"No one is comfortable with the idea of people messing with their brains. The idea that the brain is protected from medicules is a misunderstanding we spread quite deliberately. If you looked through all the literature on medicule technology, I'm sure you would find enough pieces to put it together yourself. This is publicly available information too. We just altered the flow of data and buried those papers in a pile of other research, where they would never draw unwanted attention. The problem wasn't the blood-brain barrier to begin with. All we had to do to get past that was dress our medicules up to look like the oxygen and protein that were already passing through the barrier, and we were through in no time at all. The problem, Tuan, was with the very direction of our research."

I wondered what he meant. "Personally, I see a big problem with the whole idea of controlling peoples' wills in the first place," I told him.

"I imagined you'd say that. But think about it a little. People let medicules control their bodies every day to suppress disease. Why then shouldn't we suppress potentially harmful thoughts in the brain?"

    <confusion>

       I was about to say the words "free will," but I hesitated.

       Humanity had always gone out of its way to suppress nature.

       We built cities, built societies, built systems.

       All of these revealed an overriding human desire to take the unpredictable elements of nature and place them within a predictable, controllable framework. In order to live through an age of nuclear fallout and plagues, we had striven to conquer the last remaining vestiges of nature within us, and had largely succeeded. We installed medicules in our bodies and linked up to health supervision servers. We thoroughly rid our society of lifestyle habits that were bad for our health. Our victory was complete, with the exception of old age, of course.

Wasn't the brain also part of the body? What possible reason could there be not to control it as well? I lost my conviction and sat down on the sandy riverbank. My gaze wandered off down the river. In the distance, I saw several young boys playing with a dog.

If that dog had a will of its own, then how could we say our souls are any more valuable than the soul of that dog?

```
</confusion>
```

"To our elders who lived through the Maelstrom, human will was nothing more than our barbaric nature, red in tooth and claw. Admedistrative society calls on its constituents to always remember public virtue and resource awareness. To follow its regulations and 'atmosphere' of their own free will. That is how we have been able to create the least lethal, most equal, most peaceful, and most love-filled society since the dawn of time."

The smells of the market floated down from the street to the Tigris banks.

```
<list:meal>
    <m: the sliced-open, grilled fish I just
    ate—masgouf>
    <m: the chicken breast teshreeb>
    <m: the roasted lamb quzi>
    <m: the skewered mutton kebab>
</list>
```

Smells we had excised from our society.

The kind of society my father was talking about was the society Miach hated. To her, the heights mankind had reached, this temple to peace, thoughtfulness, and health, was just another prison to be shut down and abandoned.

What a picture our society painted: everybody binding themselves to unwritten rules, carefully staying inside unseen boundaries.

I don't give a shit about love.

Or a damn about thoughtfulness.

And resource awareness can go fuck itself.

My body isn't here for the admedistration. It's not here for any of you. It's only here for me.

These tits, this ass, these belong to Miach Mihie.

Miach put my feelings into words perfectly. Or maybe my feelings changed to fit her words. Whichever it was, a part of me buried deep down still felt that way.

All I had done by getting my job as a Helix agent, besides finding a place where I could relax and smoke a cigarette in the gray zone between barbarism and morality known as the battlefield, was create a weak partition between myself and society. I had to get close to the battles to escape the suffocation of society, but I never took it all the way. I wasn't about to strap on a rifle and join in the battles myself.

I had merely found a comfortable spot somewhere between Miach and society.

Even without the mass simultaneous suicides, admedistration reports showed the suicide rate among youngsters going up year after year. More kids were

```
<list:action>
    <a: cutting their wrists.>
    <a: hanging themselves.>
    <a: jumping off buildings.>
</list>
```

Souls in danger of being crushed by society were, in turn, gnawing away at its underbelly.

Souls that just didn't fit. Souls of children yearning for disease, for damage, for pain. With wickedness in their hearts they tried to ruin their own precious lives, and they knew what they were doing. Something had to be wrong with this picture. Even in our brainwashed society, I think people had begun to realize it, but not with such clarity that they felt they could talk about the wrongness yet. It was just a slight feeling of discomfort, which they pushed down into their subconscious with all their might.

What I had found was middle ground between chaos and regulation, a limbo where I could hang for eternity.

I had sometimes felt like I was Miach's doppelgänger.

But that wasn't true at all. I had merely become the person I imagined Miach *would* have become if she had to live in my world.

"The reason I took Miach was, for one, because she was a perfect confluence of the various stressors our society creates. If we could bend Miach's obdurate will and steer it off its collision course with death, then we could control anybody. That was the thought. In those days, we picked up a lot of kids like her and put them into treatment. We gathered the ones that wanted to kill themselves—especially the ones who overate or refused to eat, the ones who wanted to watch themselves grow weak and die. Our goal was to create a harmonized will inside the human brain. We called it the Harmony program. The experiments we performed on kids like Miach were tests-to-destruction, of a sort. We were seeing how far Harmony could go."

I felt an irrational anger swelling up inside me. But not because of the tests they performed on Miach.

I wanted to know why they hadn't tested me.

Of course, I knew precisely why. They needed someone who was really, deeply, fundamentally without hope. They probably had their eyes on hundreds of emergency morality centers. There were plenty of kids back then who had attempted suicide more than once, just as there were plenty of them now.

With Miach, my father had found his rock bottom.

He had seen the despair in her eyes.

He saw that she was, as Cian had said, standing on the edge of a cliff.

That was what my father had to control, or at least attempt to control.

<anger>

>That was the reason he had abandoned me and my mother and come here to Baghdad. I had to accept that. Yes, I was feeling jealous. Children always got upset when they weren't chosen for something. Still, at the same time, what they had done was beyond grotesque.
>
>Despairing kids by the dozen.

</anger>

"How could you?"

My father nodded grimly. "It wasn't easy. But if we didn't do something, those children were a grave danger to themselves. All of them had repeatedly tried to take their own lives, and one day, they very well might have succeeded."

"Nice try, but you're just taking a consequence and calling it an objective."

"True enough. Nor were our results by any means perfect."

"What do you mean?"

"Harmony had a very serious side effect we didn't anticipate— though, in hindsight, some simple logical reasoning should have made it obvious. As it was, we never saw it coming."

Suddenly, it occurred to me what he was going to say.

He was right. Logically speaking, it was obvious. If the feed-back web reached perfect harmony and all decisions could be made without any conflict and all actions taken clearly, what would that mean? It would mean nothing less than "I" was on the line.

"You killed consciousness."

06

The death of consciousness.

My father's eyes opened wide. For moment, he seemed at a loss for words.

"That's right. How did you know?"

"Because I've heard from three people now what consciousness really is."

The answer came out so smoothly it surprised even myself.

"That's right, the conference. If all the participants have the same opinion, and all of their roles are perfectly aligned, then why hold a conference at all? If the feedback web does not plot our values on a hyperbola, but instead uses a logical, exponential curve, this is perfect harmony, in other words a state without any consciousness. It was something we couldn't detect in our tests on animals."

So my father had been trying to create a self-evident person, perfectly adapted to the stresses of admedistrative society. For someone whose every desire was self-evident, there was no need to make decisions. If their feedback web worked on clear, logical values, no will was needed to choose between one thing or the other. Consciousness was no longer required.

It almost made me laugh to think that such an obvious outcome hadn't occurred to anyone in my father's research group.

The mingled smells of spices and things cooking floated down toward the river from the direction of Abū-Nuwās. I spotted the boys again with their dog, running in and out of the water.

"We announced our findings to the other researchers and investors in the working group, that perfect harmony invariably meant the absence of consciousness. That consciousness was indeed only a mechanism for choosing between the various agents of desire teeming in our subconscious, the result of conflicts that required conscious thought to resolve, and the acting upon those conflicts. These choices were obvious to a perfectly harmonious will, thereby removing the need for a will to determine actions.

We were chasing after the perfect human but ended up killing consciousness, for it was no longer needed."

It was ironic. Our souls were nothing more than the product of a hyperbolic evaluation system we had developed over the course of our evolution. Perfect humans didn't need souls.

"What happens when you lose your consciousness? Do you just sit there all day in your chair, drooling?"

"Nothing of the sort. You go shopping, you eat, you enjoy entertainment—you merely no longer have to make decisions what to do at any given time because everything is self-evident. It's the difference between having to make choices and having it all be obvious to you. That's all it is. That's what divides the world of the consciousness and the world without. People have absolutely no problem living without consciousness or will, Tuan. They live their lives as normal. People can be born, grow old, and die without consciousness. Consciousness has very little to do with culture, really. From the outside, it's nearly impossible to tell whether someone has a consciousness or is merely *acting* as though they did. However, because their system of values is fashioned to be in perfect harmony with society, there are far fewer suicides, and the kinds of stress we find in our admedistrative society disappear completely."

So Miach and presumably these other kids had experienced this in the tests. They had experienced *being* without a consciousness.

All the billions of people on this earth had, at some point in their ancestry, along the long path of evolution, obtained what we call a consciousness. Evolution was a very haphazard thing. Only the genes well suited to a particular environment survived. The result of these patched-together adaptations was the species of human as we knew it now, each one of us possessing that curious byproduct of evolution we called a consciousness.

"When she came back, Miach said it had been pure ecstasy," my father said with a wry chuckle. "While she was without consciousness, she ate normally, studied, spoke with us, and lived life as normal. When we brought her consciousness back, Miach didn't remember a thing about her time during the test. She only had the sensation that she had been in a wonderful, joyous place."

That made sense to me. You couldn't look at dogs and not think they were, generally speaking, much happier than people. Someone once said that the bird that freezes upon the branch never knows suffering. What Miach had experienced was the state of mankind long before we had obtained consciousness, long before we got lost in the labyrinthine world of introspection and reflection.

The sun was sinking below the horizon now. I reached out as if to touch it with my fingers. People with perfect judgment do not require a consciousness, so it does not exist.

"And you tried to do this to everyone in the world? You were going to steal consciousness from everyone who was stupid enough to install WatchMe?"

"No—we weren't," my father said, beginning to walk back up the bank in the direction of the street. "We could not just make the decision to eliminate consciousness. For one, I was terrified of the thought. To lose who I am, my own consciousness…In a sense, it's like dying. We didn't have the right to decide whether or not to impose something like that on billions of people."

"I suppose it depends on what death is," I said.

I admit that I shared an inclination to think of my *self* as my consciousness. The consciousness had the ability to make predictions and to control and order the body and mind, and it was easy to think of that as being everything. Though I was sure my body saw things differently.

We were back in the heat of the crowd up on the main street. Lights had gone on, bare bulbs illuminating the open shop fronts. It wasn't just restaurants—there were places selling cooking wares and fabrics and carpets. People of different occupations bustled about in the midst of mingled smells from the many stoves and grills.

"We asked WHO and a few of the admedistrations to make a decision," my father was saying. "In the end, we settled on a compromise, that we would install the system in everyone, but not activate it. That's right, the medicule network necessary to control our feedback web is already in place in your brain, as it is in mine. If ever mankind should threaten to sink back into the chaos that was the Maelstrom, then, as an emergency measure, we can activate Harmony."

```
<anger>
```
Praise be to God. Though none of us asked, we have received. An automatic hallelujah device in our brains. Stuck right onto the synapses of our midbrain, never to let go or be removed. I could hear the choir singing now.
```
<music:name=Messiah:id=2y6r58jnjhu7451110eo99>
    <Hallelujah!>
    <Hallelujah!>
    <Hallelujah!>
    <Hallelujah!>
    <Hallelujah!>
</music>
```
Ever since God had given us our self-awareness, it had done nothing but torment the suicidal and the literary among us, and now we were free to throw it all away. Free to return in primal ecstasy to the Kingdom of Heaven.
Hallelujah.
```
</anger>
```

"So you gave someone the power of life and death over our consciousnesses and stole Miach's consciousness away from her? You're worse than I thought."

"I thought you'd say something of the sort—though admittedly, I never expected to hear that from the despairing little girl you used to be. I'm sure most people wouldn't want to lose that part of their brain that recognizes 'me' as 'me.' No matter what the potential cost to society. Which is why the old folks in our group, in their fear of the chaos that was the Maelstrom, put their plan into action without any public discussion or any morality session review."

If these old folks wanted it, the human race could have its consciousness taken away.

We could all become people free of our useless consciousness, all doing precisely what we should be doing at all times.

We could upgrade to the newer model. *Homo perfectus.*

"So if you wanted to—"

"Yes, but right now, we do not. No matter how big a mountain of suicides our gentle society creates, there has to be a societal solution for this. Because we believe this, our fingers have never once strayed toward the Harmony button. Believe me, we don't want this to happen."

"But Miach Mihie does?"

My father stopped and picked up a kettle from a stand out in front of one of the shops. He stared at it. "Tuan. Have you ever heard of the island of sign language?"

I blinked and said that I hadn't. "That's kind of a sudden change of topic, don't you think?"

"The people who first colonized Martha's Vineyard—that's an island off the American coast—were cut off for some time from the mainland, and there was a lot of inbreeding. This resulted in several families where both parents had a recessive gene for deafness, and in another generation or two, hardly anyone on the island could hear at all. It was more unusual to *have* your hearing than not. So, everyone on the island communicated via sign language. Sign language became their mother tongue. And no one was the worse for it. There, a person with hearing—which we take to be the norm—was instead a radical departure from the norm. Their culture did not require a sense of sound."

"I'm still not sure what this has to do with our conversation."

"It has to do with Miach Mihie."

"Don't tell me that she was deaf—or wait, that she had some sort of consciousness impairment, like those people had a hearing impairment?"

"No, she had a consciousness. However, it was different from ours in that she had formed her consciousness sometime after her birth."

<shaken>

After her birth?

"You mean, she was born *without* a consciousness?"

"That's correct." My father tapped the kettle he held with one fingernail. *Ding.* The clear, high tone echoed in my skull. "Several decades ago, in the midst of the conflict between Russia and Chechnya, a minority ethnic group was discovered. This was a completely new group as far as the scientific community was concerned, mind you, not appearing in any records until then. Though their clothing, food, culture, and language had all been influenced by the surrounding peoples, they avoided close relations with any of them, maintaining a small community in a rugged mountainous region, where they had been inbreeding for many generations."

"Wait, Dad, are you saying—"

"I'm saying that these people shared a common recessive trait. It's a trait that shows up very rarely in the general population, and the chances of two people with it marrying are so slim that there has never been any observations made of this occurring. The trait of which I speak is a missing gene—the gene responsible for consciousness. I'm sure that of the billions of people in the world, there are a few born without the ability to form a consciousness, but in this Chechen minority group, nearly everyone lacked a consciousness."

"But then how did they live or develop a culture?"

"After we found them, we ran them through several tests. They were extremely adept at logical thinking. Their value system was not like our irrational hyperbola, which attributes too much value to that which is right before us. They did not make choices. MRI scans showed that, indeed, there was none of the activity we associate with consciousness going on, yet they lived regular lives and had their own culture—though much of it was borrowed from surrounding peoples as the need arose. They were a people that neither possessed nor required consciousness. Just like the people of Martha's Vineyard didn't require speech. They were people in perfect harmony with a perfectly logical value system."

"So Miach..."

"The conflict had spread into the mountains, plunging her people into chaos. Miach was taken from her village at the age of eight by Russian soldiers and sent to a camp run by human traffickers. This was a place of unspeakable tragedy, where sex slaves were kept for the sole use of the Russian army. This is where her consciousness awoke. Her brain needed a consciousness with a hyperbolic value system in order to withstand the daily, immediate terror of repeated rape. What happened was, a region in her cerebrum began to emulate the functions of the feedback mechanism usually handled by the midbrain. You've heard stories of how brains damaged in accidents will activate undamaged regions to take over some of the lost functionality, right? The brain is a very flexible organ."

Miach's consciousness was an emulation?

Not a true consciousness like our own.

Not a pattern woven by the feedback web in the midbrain.

A replica, created to serve a dire need.

Imitation consciousness.

I stared at my father's back. He hadn't brought Miach to Baghdad just because her despair had been deeper and more violent than mine.

He had brought her here because of her lineage.

So she had been dragged from hell to start a new life in

Japan, but for Miach, that wasn't harmony either. Japan's society, in its attempt to attain a kind of harmony, let itself be ruled by a strangling, enforced kindness that had produced a mountain of suicides.

Miach Mihie hated admedistrative society as much as she had hated Chechnya.

For Miach, Chechnya and Tokyo were just two different neighborhoods in the same hell.

</shaken>

Had Miach wanted to take us with her into death because she saw harmony on the other side?

"There are always monsters who find sexual attraction in children. These pedophiles among the Russian soldiers forced her to develop a consciousness out of hate, or rather something like a consciousness, and her newfound simulated consciousness despaired and chose death. I found it profoundly moving, and discouraging, that the decision to end one's own life is a high-level, conscious act, that only one with a conflicted consciousness can make."

Dong! Just then, the kettle my father was holding flew out of his hands.

It shot across the shop, barely missing the half-dozing shop-keeper before crashing into a pile of pots and pans.

I whirled around and spotted a man hiding beneath a large hat. He was about ten feet away, smoke still rising from the barrel of his gun. Vashlov. The gun was pointed toward us.

"Interpol," he said, reaching in with his free hand to pull a business card from his breast pocket. "Pleased to make your acquaintance, Dr. Nuada Kirie. I'm also pleased to inform you that you're under arrest for the mass coercion of suicides."

<tension>

I took a step back, my hand reaching for the gun beneath my jacket.

"Whoa there, Tuan. You don't move either. You're related to the accused, after all."

"Liar," I said.

"No really, you are related to him. Or did you mean something else?"

I spat on the ground. "You're not Interpol."

"Oh, but I am. Look, it's written on my card." He waved his card in the air. Seeing the lack of reaction on our faces, he frowned. "Aw. And I thought my cards would be a big hit, what with AR off-line here."

"You may have Interpol ID, but you're working for Miach's group, against my father. You've been at the center of this madness all along."

"An intriguing deduction."

I took another half step back, further into the shop. "You figured that by putting me into play you could get my father out in the open, away from the protection of the Next-Gen group."

"Fascinating. And what was I going to do then?" Vashlov grinned, clearly enjoying himself. My right hand moved toward the holster again, and his gun jerked up to point straight at me. "I really wouldn't do that, Miss. It's not necessary. I'm only here to take Dr. Kirie into my custody."

"I don't suppose taking him back to Geneva is part of the plan."

"Probably not. I am, as you say, with Miach Mihie."

"What do you want?"

"Your father is the leader of the main faction within our group, you see." The barrel drifted over to point at my father. "If I take him in, they'll lose their focus—it will *weaken* them. The next day or two are of vital importance, you see. If I can keep him out of action just a little while, the balance of things will shift in a favorable direction."

"And what direction might that be?"

"Well, we—"

While Vashlov was talking—a bit too involved with what he was saying—I had reached behind me with my left hand until I found a smallish metal object with a handle. Now I threw it at him as hard as I could. The pot smacked Vashlov's forehead with a dull *thonk* and he lost his footing, falling over backwards. I almost laughed out loud at the unexpected efficacy of my attack.

```
</tension>
```

"Dad! This way!" I pulled my father's hand toward the night street, hoping to lose ourselves in the crowd.

"Stop right there, Kiries! Both of you!"

We had made it about thirty feet by the time Vashlov got to his feet, blood trickling from a gash in his forehead. Not that thirty feet is very far to travel when you're a bullet. If there weren't people on the road between us, we would have been dead already.

"Stay close to me," I told my father.

He nodded. "We have to do something—"

I pulled him by the hand again, pushing our way farther through the crowd. Our progress was made more difficult by the fact that I had no idea where we were going. If I had my AR on, and it was linked up to StreetWatch, I would know where every side street led to before we got to it. Running in an unfamiliar place in an unfamiliar land without AR was like running a race blindfolded.

"I said stop!" I heard Vashlov shouting behind us.

Sorry, pal.

We ran ahead, dodging a cart filled with fish for making *masgouf.* This place was chaos, filled with the smells of nutmeg, cardamom, cinnamon, cumin seeds, perfume, and the bodily odors and bad breath of people without the benefit of WatchMe. Most of the men here were construction laborers who commuted into the medical industrial complex sector to work on the next giant building site. I looked behind me as we ran, but

without AR, I had no idea where Vashlov might be hiding in
the crowd.

"Sorry!"

We'd reached the restaurant where I'd eaten earlier that evening. I turned, pulling my father along behind me. Ignoring the
accented complaint of the proprietor we ran through the shop,
kicking through two sets of doors until we were outside again
in an alleyway behind the restaurant.

Vashlov was standing no more than ten feet away from us,
off to one side, facing right toward us.

```
<tension>
<silence>
```
    In a moment of frozen time, Vashlov and I lifted our
guns to point at one another.

    Two shots were fired.

    One from my gun.

    One from Vashlov's.

    Both of them hit their targets.
```
</silence>
</tension>
```

Target No. 1: Vashlov's chest.

Target No. 2: My father's chest.

"Dad!"

```
<mourning>
```
    My father had stepped out in front of me, between me
and the barrel of Vashlov's gun. As if he were trying to
make up for thirteen years of lost parenting with a single
act. And now he was dead. I put my hand to his neck but
couldn't get a warm pulse anywhere.

    I had no tears. Inhuman, you think?

    It was like the thirteen years had erased the father from
my father. My sadness was a far gentler, quieter thing than

what I had felt at Cian's death or even at the first "death," which had been Miach's. In thirteen years, my father had become a stranger, with nothing to identify him to me, save the unseen, encoded ties of blood between us.

But it hadn't been that way for him, had it. He had abandoned me and gone off with Miach to his own medical mecca. Yet he had still loved his daughter, even as I felt hardly anything for him at all. Perhaps his stepping in front of me had not been a conscious act but a reflexive one encoded in his DNA. Maybe that was the love I lacked—the love for one's family.

My father had died for me, so now the only way I could repay him was with gratitude.

"Thank you."

</mourning>

I reached down and smoothed my father's half-opened eyelids shut, then stood, listening to the wheezing sound coming from Vashlov's windpipe. He would be joining my father soon, but if he were still alive, I had plenty of things I wanted to ask him first.

"My father is dead. I hope you're happy."

"Works for me," he said quietly. "I was hoping to abduct—but death is a big win too. Thanks to you sniffing around we managed to drag him out. Finally got Nuada…They'll have a hard time putting things together now. Very hard. General chaos will take care of the rest."

"What is it that you want?"

"What do we want? To build a new, post-chaos world. To bring an enduring harmony…"

There was something very disturbing about a group claiming they wanted peace when they had just plunged the world into darkness with a wave of suicides, and then, in the greatest act of terror in history, demanded the survivors kill each other.

"I don't see a whole lot of harmony out there right now."

"Things will settle down, as they must. This chaos is merely a step on the path toward peace. Miach Mihie has shown us the way. She is our prophet. She has a vision for mankind…the right path for us to take. You know her from when you were a child. You know that she can see what is yet to come."

"So she had to make six thousand people try to kill themselves for this future?"

"Yes."

"I'm sorry, but that's not very convincing." I grabbed him by the collar. "Where's Miach?"

I could see blood seeping from Vashlov's chest with every breath. He had lost a lot already. I must've hit a big artery or vein in there. Some of it was getting into his lungs, making it hard for him to breathe. His voice was a whisper, forced out through something that sounded just like I imagined a death rattle would sound.

"The suicides and the threats are just…the catalyst. Things are already in motion. But if you must know, Miach told me I could tell you where she was—but you have to promise to shoot me in the head if I tell you."

Vashlov's lips thinned and he formed a warped smile. For a moment, I hesitated.

A pleading look came into his eyes. "This really hurts. It *hurts*. Th-this is what pain feels like. WatchMe and medcare, you bastards, you sure did a fine job of keeping me in the dark about this sensation. Doesn't that piss you off, Miss Kirie? Please…"

"Fine. Deal."

I put the barrel of my gun to Vashlov's forehead and pulled back the hammer. It clicked into place with a satisfying metallic sound and Vashlov breathed out with relief.

"Chechnya. Check with the Anti-Russian Freedom Front in Chechnya."

"What, Miach is *there*?"

"You'll just have to go see for yourself."

Vashlov nodded to signal he was ready.

Something about the way his eyes looked through me made

my finger pause, motionless, on the trigger. Here, beneath the rapidly darkening Iraq sky, I was about to kill someone for the first time in my life. Right here, in this very moment. I was making the same decision that had been forced on billions of people across the world.

This would free me from having to make that choice in a few days, I realized. It felt like cheating. The guy was begging me to do it, and I would even be avenging my father's death. You couldn't make up a better rationale than that. I steadied my grip on the gun and felt intense self-loathing.

A thought occurred to me. Why had my brain developed this function it was expressing now? In what environment would self-loathing give me an evolutionary advantage?

I pulled the trigger.

```
</body>
</etml>
```

<part:number=04:title=The Day the World Went Away/>

```
<?Emotion-in-Text Markup Language:version=1.2:enc
oding=EMO-590378?>
<!DOCTYPE etml PUBLIC :-//WENC//DTD ETML 1.2
transitional//EN>
//<etml:lang=jp>
<etml:lang=en>
<body>
```

01

<recollection>

The three of us were sitting on a rooftop, each with our own lunch. The contents of mine and Cian's had both been decided by our mothers based on a range of choices provided them by a lifestyle pattern designer to ensure a perfect balance of nutritional control and modest tastes—so as not to overexcite our youthful minds with shameful flavors.

All our mothers had to do was make the food.

The flavors we needed were determined by a specially trained lifestyle pattern designer who could read our bodies' preferences and predilections. The designer then ordered all the necessary ingredients online, coordinating with our household management software to make sure our diets stayed within budget.

The various facets of our lives were being divided into smaller and smaller sections. Outsourcing, outsourcing,

outsourcing. When I was very small, I had the feeling that things weren't quite so scattered. I was pretty sure I remembered my mom fretting about my age and height and weight and body fat percentage when I was around five years old. She would read charts, size me up, and come up with her own lunch recipes.

Miach's lunch was nothing like ours. The recipes were incredibly simple, and more than two-thirds of her rather large lunch box would be filled with white rice and a big reddish-black lump in the middle of it that I think was probably an *umeboshi* pickled plum.

"Naoya Shiga used to say that the Japanese lost the war because they ate white rice," Miach said, her cheeks full of white rice laced with sesame salt. A single grain of rice was stuck to her cheek.

"What war?"

"The Second World War. It was a fight between the two nations of America and Japan."

"But didn't both of them get divided up by the admedistrations?"

"Right, but this was back when America was still a country. Before the Maelstrom."

"Um, Miach, that's great, but you have rice on your face," Cian broke in, giggling.

"Oh." Miach found it with her index finger and plucked it off.

"Why do you eat so much all the time, Miach?"

"Because I like to eat. And if I don't eat this much, my head doesn't work right."

I looked between my lunch and Miach's. "You don't have many things besides rice in there. It's mostly all rice. And your lunch box is huge too."

"Yet I'm skinny. Funny, isn't it? The brown adipose tissue on my back did a number on my metabolism. I burn everything and none of the food gets to my brain.

That's why I have to shove so much of it in. If there was a speed-eating contest, I bet I'd win it."

"What's that?"

"These contests where people would try to see who could eat the most the fastest. The media channels used to show things like that, before the Maelstrom. It's all shockingly unhealthy. The kind of thing those people in morality sessions love to bad-mouth."

It sounded pretty horrible. I didn't see how there could be any pleasure in damaging your stomach and intestines by eating so much. I sat down on the rooftop, looking down on city streets devoid of any shapes or colors that might prove too stimulating. "So, what do you tell your mom or dad what you want to eat for lunch?"

"I don't. That is, I make my lunch myself. Of course my mom wants me to use this nosy lifestyle pattern designer or something. No thanks."

"Doesn't it reflect poorly on your mom's SA score if her daughter doesn't take her health advice?"

"Maybe. Or maybe not. I'm never really sure about those things. You know the old saying, 'Kids grow up despite their parents.'"

"Yeah, but isn't it a little different? I thought it went: 'Even without parents, children will flourish.'"

"Yes, that's the original. But there was this writer named Ango Sakaguchi, and he said that children would flourish *without* the useless baggage that is their parents. That's a lot different than saying a kid's going to grow up even without the benefit of parents. Of course, a lot of people have different ideas as to what constitutes flourishing."

"Sakaguchi, huh? Sounds interesting."

"You can download it from the Borgesnet. I recommend actually reading it—you know, with your eyes—instead of using the reader."

So saying, Miach picked up a large lump of rice sprinkled

with sesame salt and crammed it into her mouth. The sight of her chewing with both cheeks full was so comical I had to laugh.

"What?"

"Do you really have to cram it all in at once like that?"

"I'm just trying to match you guys. You have so much less that if I don't eat quick, I'll never keep up."

"Don't worry about keeping up with me," Cian said. "I always leave some anyway." She closed her lunch box with an audible snap. "My parents want me to eat it, but it's way too much for the middle of the day."

"Oh yeah?"

"Yeah. I mean, I don't really get hungry until two or three o'clock. At noon I still feel full from breakfast."

"Do you know why we eat lunch at noon?" Miach asked through a full mouth.

I shrugged. "Is it because we're hungry?"

"Apparently Cian isn't."

I looked in Cian's direction, then lowered my head. "Oh, right. Sorry."

"That's okay, you don't have to apologize."

"Neither of you do," Miach joined in. "People get hungry whenever they feel like it, that's natural. It's that the school system doesn't approve of natural human flexibility."

"Well, if you're going to have a group of people eating, it makes sense to eat together."

"Why can't we eat during class is what I want to know."

Now that she mentioned it, it did seem curious that people often read or watched media channels while they were eating, but we weren't supposed to eat while we read our textbooks in school. Maybe it was because it would distract us from class? But that didn't make sense either. Class and lunch were equally boring. At least, my mother's lunches never tasted good enough to distract me from anything.

"It's a rule. These rules are meant to divide up our time,

partition it, control it. Strictly speaking, by getting hungry around two or three o'clock, Cian's digestive system is going against the rules—and Cian blames her own body for not being able to get with the program. She blames herself. How silly is that?"

Miach was in the zone now. Miach, our ideologue. She gathered up another ball of rice with her chopsticks, still talking. "The time divisions at school have been the same for a long while. What started as the idea that it was fun for everyone to eat together, or that it made more sense for work, eventually became proscribed in more detail, with start times and end times. It became a rule. You know there was no such thing as lifestyle pattern designers before lifeism took off? But once something like that becomes popular, it becomes the thing to do, then it becomes a rule, then it becomes law. Just another of the invisible things out there trying to control our bodies."

Miach kept talking at full speed, her cheeks full of a lot of rice and a little bit of toppings. Finally she tossed back the last bit of rice, packed up her lunch box, and put it back in her bag. Then she stood and walked over to the railing that ran around the rooftop and spoke out loud, like she was making a proclamation to the scenery—or even to the entire world.

"'It is over life, throughout its unfolding, that power establishes its dominion; death is power's limit, the moment that escapes it; death becomes the most secret aspect of existence, the most "private."'"

"Who said that?"

"Michel Foucault."

Even though her lunch was much bigger than ours, Miach had finished way before we were done. I ate up the last of mine, wrapped my lunch box in a cloth, and tucked it away inside my bag. A quiet breeze blew, brushing past our foreheads and through our hair.

Death is power's limit, the moment that escapes it.

"So is that the only way out?" I asked quietly.

Miach was looking out over the city, confronting it. "I used to be in another place, under the dominion of another power. It was hell," she said without turning around. "That's why I escaped, to come here. But here's crazy too. This is no place for people to live."

"What was it like, the other place?"

"The exact opposite of here. Over there guns kill people. Here, kindness kills them. It's all the same."

</recollection>

So here I was, thirteen years later, in that other place Miach had told us about.

Already, several small-scale disturbances had broken out across the globe. The police forces, accustomed to the peaceful routine of everyday life, were immediately overloaded, and many cities and admedistrations had gone weeping to those few remaining countries with standing militaries to beg for assistance.

<movie:ar:id=6aehko908724h3008k>
<fear>

Franz Recht picked up the knife his wife always used and looked at it.

It was the knife she used to cut cabbage for her sauerkraut.

The knife she used to slice blutwurst.

Franz Recht had never been very good at cooking. He had left all that to her. He would clean up around the house and go shopping, but he had never cooked a single meal. It had been a long time since he had even set foot in the kitchen.

Once he had stepped in though, his eyes had started to swim. Perhaps he was dazed by the sheer variety of potentially lethal items he found there. Practically any of them would suit his current purpose. Which made sense, when he thought about it. This was a place for ending and processing life.

Cutting, carving, beating, burning, stewing, steaming. Many religions have rules about food.

```
<dictionary>
      <item>Kosher</item>
<definition>
```

Dietary restrictions followed by those of the Jewish faith. As blood is life, goes one teaching, the blood must be removed from food in the proper manner. A strict observer's kitchen will have two sinks. One to drain the blood and purify the food, the other for typical kitchen use. Pork, considered to never be clean, is prohibited.

```
</definition>

      <item>Halal<item>
<definition>
```

Tenets of Islam, especially those pertaining to food. *Halal* literally means "that which is permitted by Allah." All meat must be slaughtered according to the method called *dhabiha* if it is to be halal. Dhabiha requires that you use a sharp knife to cut the windpipe, esophagus, and carotid artery swiftly, so as to cause the animal as little pain as possible, while leaving the spinal cord intact. The preparer then says "*Bismillah Allahu akbar*" to ask for Allah's blessing, and only then is the meat considered to be halal.

```
</definition>
</dictionary>
```

This was the way food used to be. Only consumed after all the necessary, annoying protocol had been followed.

That was how killing was too.

"Honey!"

A call from the door. Franz's wife was home. His eyes went to the entranceway. Franz went down the hall to greet his wife just inside the door, where he plunged the carving knife he had just picked up in the kitchen into her chest.

Being a rather moderate Christian, Franz had no need for halal or dhabiha. He certainly wasn't going to say *Allahu akbar*. He just had to thrust out with his arm to bury the knife—the one she used to cut the cabbage for her sauerkraut—into her rib cage.

Her eyes met his in surprise.

Perhaps he was frightened, or perhaps—being an amateur at this—he wasn't sure how much force was necessary to actually kill, or whether he had managed to hit a vital organ. So to be safe, Franz knelt over his fallen wife and stabbed her again and again. He stabbed her in the chest and the stomach and everywhere except her head, that head with the beautiful face. He kept stabbing for several minutes until her body was in ribbons.

</fear>

Then Franz put a hand to one ear and called the police, while he was still straddling his wife's corpse. *Yes, I just killed my wife. Yes. You know, what they were saying, how we had to kill someone or we would die? I figured there's no death penalty in this country. And I don't mean to be demanding, but could you please send a patrol car to pick me up? What? They're all out? I see, well I suppose everyone is busy these days. Busy like me.*

Franz hung up the phone and stared at the body beneath him for a few moments before he began to weep.

</movie>

"And that's just one example," Stauffenberg was saying.

Everyone participating in the AR session was standing, stunned, wherever they happened to be in the real world.

"It appears the declaration started to take hold in earnest yesterday. We've had other killings and many suicides as well. Even with the gag order on the media, everyone seems to be getting the same idea."

Someone asked what the admedistrations were doing.

Stauffenberg shook her head. "Those admedistrations with enough wherewithal to hire civilian police forces have sent them all out already. In addition, at the general assembly of the admedistrations, they made a request for national police forces and armies and, if possible, Geneva Convention forces to be placed in every city, but it's already getting difficult to find available troops, and many places are already too destabilized to help. Riots and lawlessness are spreading. It is, in fact, looking like the second coming of the Maelstrom, at least to hear the older folks tell it. No place is safe. Kill another, kill yourself, or be killed. It's the perfect recipe for chaos."

Different images flickered on the virtual screen. A pile of bloody corpses, thirty high, resting on a cobblestone street in some typical European village. Medical troops wearing pink gas masks were adding bodies to the pile, trying to clear a path for vehicles to pass. Another clip showed men and women breaking through barricades, wielding sticks and pipes against the army; the troops turned to using nonlethal microwaves to keep them back. The rioters would just run off in some other direction. No matter what the soldiers did, it was ineffective.

"The day after tomorrow is the deadline, so to speak. Fear has swallowed many already, and it will get worse."

A satellite image showed a group of half-dressed men in a circle around two combatants wielding knives, caught by the satellite's cold gaze. The men around were urging on the two in the middle. Once each of them had killed one other person, the group would disperse. If men had the rational capacity to make rules for killing like this, how could they lack the rational ability to choose not to believe the declaration and let the deadline come? Our hyperbolic valuing system overestimated the clear and present fear, driving us to illogical action.

We were breaking open the piggy bank with money still in our wallets.

"There are, at present, no reports of any murders within our police or military forces. However, I would not be much surprised if those reports came—merely disheartened."

"Even if the killer was a Helix agent?" I asked with dark sarcasm in my voice.

Prime's lips thinned, and a twisted smile came to her face. "Yes, even then. I fully intend to stay at my post until the moment of reckoning, as I believe all of you will choose to do, but with such chaos before us, I can understand if you are finding your resolve tested. Not that I'm worried about you, Agent Kirie. You've already killed someone, haven't you."

"In self-defense."

"Lucky for you. Must be nice to kill without feeling guilt."

"Shouldn't we be talking about the investigation?" I asked, countering Stauffenberg's sarcasm with duty. Prime nodded quietly and motioned for me to continue.

"This gets a little complicated, but bear with me. The man I killed was a member of Interpol, yet he was using his authority as such for the benefit of a secret society to which he belonged. His name was Elijah Vashlov. I have confirmed that he was on staff at Interpol HQ as an intelligence regulator. Intel regulators are responsible for sifting through the fractured intelligence relating to crimes that cross between the jurisdiction of multiple governments and/or admedistrations, and help negotiate information-sharing protocols."

"Which is why he showed up both in Japan and in Baghdad."

"That's right. The secret society for which he worked is called the Next-Gen Human Behavior Monitoring Group. This group was launched soon after the Maelstrom ended and consists of top people in the admedistrations, medical industrial collectives, the upper echelon of WHO, and a handful of independent scientists. I was unable to obtain more information than this from Vashlov. According to the information I did obtain, this group's primary objective is to prevent global chaos like the Maelstrom from ever happening again. Toward this end, they had enlisted the help of neuromedical researchers."

"Can you explain this research?"

"They're looking into the connection between human will and human action. I'm no expert on the subject, so that's about as far as I got."

"And then you killed the man who gave you this information?"

"My father was also killed. By Vashlov," I replied, straining to keep my anger in check.

"That's right. I hear he took a bullet for you. Can you explain why you went to meet with your father?"

"Because I had heard he was part of the Next-Gen group. My father is a famous scientist, the one who first postulated the basic theory that made WatchMe and medcare a possibility. It seemed not at all unlikely that such a group would call for his services."

"Yet that doesn't make sense. If everything you have told us is true, that would mean that this Vashlov fellow killed your father even though they were part of the same group."

I thought for a moment. Two people were dead. One of them by my hand. There was only so far I could take this without revealing something. I needed to figure out how few of my cards I could show and how far I could get away with some harmless lies in order for Stauffenberg to be satisfied.

"Within this group, there are two factions, each with different ideologies. Vashlov identified himself as a heretic within the group. I can only speculate that he was referring to this internal conflict."

"And now that your father and this Vashlov are both dead, there is nothing remaining to prove the existence of this conspiracy."

No, that wasn't true. Vashlov had told me that the SEC

Neuromedical Research Consortium was merely a public front for the Next-Gen group.

"There is one other known collaborator by the name of Gabrielle Étaín."

"Who is dead. Murdered. Three hours ago."

"What?" I gasped.

Stauffenberg was staring me down. "It was a random killing, as random as any of the killings in the world have been these last few days. It happened in broad daylight, in a corridor of the Dian Cécht complex in Baghdad. With all the scientists, who tend to be more levelheaded than the average mob, there have been fewer killings and group suicides in Baghdad—but there have been some exceptions. Within Dian Cécht alone, there have already been fourteen untimely deaths, both murders and suicides in just the last two days. Already, the casework is far beyond what security and the Baghdad police can handle."

"We could investigate the SEC?"

"We will. Though with such a vital source as Gabrielle gone, I have my doubts as to how far such an investigation would take us—where are you now, by the way?"

"In a PassengerBird. Upper deck."

"To where?"

"Chechnya."

"Why Chechnya? Another loose thread?"

"I can't say."

This was it. I could show no more of my hand. What I needed was a convenient lie.

"Vashlov told me that there were members of his group within the Helix Inspection Agency. I don't know which superiors you report to, ma'am, but I think that the chances of them being sympathizers are high."

This was my big bluff. Vashlov had said nothing of the sort. Although now that I thought about it, it did seem like an idea with some merit.

"Given a choice, I'd prefer not to telegraph our every move

to our opponent."

"You mean *your* every move. With Cian Reikado's death, and now your father's, this case has become quite personal for you, hasn't it. It doesn't bode well, Inspector Kirie."

"And yet, I have made more progress than any other agent."

Stauffenberg stared me in the eye. I couldn't read anything in her expression. Maybe she was trying to read me. Or maybe she was just trying to accept reality. After five seconds of silence, Prime asked for everyone else to leave the session. One by one, the other Helix agents logged off, scratching their heads as they went. I was alone with Stauffenberg. She took a deep breath and said, "All right. I'll be honest. It's me."

I had no idea what she was talking about.

"I'm an upper-rank member in the Next-Gen Human Behavior Monitoring Group."

I laughed out loud, both at my bluff having hit the mark so well, and at the ridiculousness of my current situation.

"So you were following me the whole time?"

"Yes. Both sides of our group have been watching you. We had given you mostly free reign in hopes that you would contact Miach Mihie's group or they you in the course of your investigation."

"So it wasn't the Tuareg card after all."

"You were allowed to continue operating for the sole purpose of tracking down Miach Mihie's whereabouts. You're not the first Helix agent to disgrace herself in the field, and your past behavior certainly wouldn't have bought you any of your current relative freedom."

So the Next-Gen group wanted Miach, and Miach's sect wanted Nuada, and both sides had been using me to get what they wanted.

"Both of you needed to track down the leader of the other group, which made me very valuable as the daughter of one and the friend of the other."

"It just happens that you and we are after the same person. We were cooperating—as unintentional as it may have been."

"It certainly does seem that way."

"I'm sorry about your father, truly."

Judging from the look on Stauffenberg's face, she was telling the truth. It wasn't hard to picture my father as a respected leader of his group. There was an ironic gap between that and my memory of him getting chewed out by that woman in the morality session all those years ago.

"Miach Mihie still possesses a limited ability to control feedback mechanisms within the brains of the constituencies of several admedistrations. She's gone into hiding. What they have been doing is manipulating the feedback mechanism within the midbrain to instill a desire for death, causing people to kill themselves. We wanted to use you to get into contact with her so we could find out what her goals were in causing this current chaos, and attempt to stop her. You see, we have absolutely no idea what she's up to."

Had it only been me and Cian, and probably my father, who knew about Miach's dark past? All those curses we dreamed up to cast on the world, huddled together at our desks on those dreary school days. Wasn't Miach still carrying the hatred she had held in her heart back then? Wasn't she just using her newfound power to put her fantasies into action—her power to make mincemeat of the society she so despised?

If that was true, then the current situation was an extremely private one for us, and now that Cian and my father were gone, I was the only one capable of understanding it.

There was a point to slowly releasing the shackles of our social system as she was doing, to using an abject fear of others to undo the little fetters around each of us one at a time—and I was the only one who got it.

A world where your body was your own. That was what the Miach I had known as a child wanted. A body that was hers, not beholden to a society or its rules.

"So, what can we do about this?" Prime asked.

"Who's the agent in charge of monitoring life-issues between

Chechnya and Russia?"

"That's...Inspector Uwe Vol."

"Then can you direct him to aid my investigation once I arrive?"

"Very well." Stauffenberg went to cut our connection, then her hand stopped. "The fate of the world is resting on your shoulders, Inspector Kirie. Good luck."

Words of personal encouragement were about the last thing I had expected from my typically venomous boss. This whole thing had started as a personal matter, and if anything, it had only gotten more personal as I went. Frankly, even with all the riots and mass suicide going on, I hadn't been worried about the world at all. All I wanted to do was find Miach Mihie—who had killed Cian, and probably my father as well—and somehow get some closure from her. That was the only thing keeping me moving, the only thing I really *felt*.

I went off-line, feeling jumpy in the pit of my stomach. I asked the flight attendant for some caffeine. Something shamefully strong, I added. I was no longer worried about appearances, and it had been a while since I had gotten a good night's sleep, so I needed the boost.

Uwe would be with the Chechen armistice monitoring group. That was where I was headed.

02

Pretty much everyone in the world knew that Russia's only real concern in the region was control of the pipeline. It was a thorn in the side of every admedistration in the world, I was sure, that we hadn't completely rid ourselves of the decidedly environmentally *un*aware oil economy. Fossil fuels

```
<list:item>
    <i: produce carbon dioxide.>
    <i: produce heat.>
```

```
<i: pollute the land and the atmosphere.>
<i: are all-around nasty stuff.>
</list>
```

Unclean, unsafe, uncool.

Still, there were classic engines around that wouldn't run without oil, and products made from oil. Compared to a hundred years earlier when the world had been in the grip of the black gold, oil had lost much of its allure, though it still clung to a vital position in the global market.

As Dubai had become an economic center thanks to the performance of the oil sector, Baghdad had vaulted to its current status as an economic powerhouse on the shoulders of the medical conglomerates. As the saying goes, trust in Allah, but be sure to tie up your camel. The Middle East had gone through a chaotic period of runaway fundamentalism before emerging into a more practical, tie-up-your-camel age. The smarter governments in the region had already begun uprooting their stakes in oil.

The old-style government of Russia remained the largest single system among the clustered admedistrations that controlled Eurasia, though this hadn't kept the admedistrations from roundly criticizing their oversized neighbor's policies when it came to control of the oil pipeline. Not a few admedistration commissioners had wondered openly why Geneva Convention forces had been pulled in to help Russia enforce its claims of ownership.

Russia, the nation, wanted war with Chechnya. Russia, the collection of admedistrations, each wanted to save the Chechens from their own unhealthy ways, and they each had different ideas as to how best to achieve their goal. This meant that Uwe was dealing with far more than just armed Chechen groups, the Chechen government, and the Russian government. There were over a hundred different admedistrations within Russia, and all of them had something to say, and all of them said it to him. Russia, eager to generate international support, had invited the Helix Inspection Agency in to investigate, whereupon they found that the Chechen people were not living sufficiently lifeist, healthy lives, which gave Russia a sufficient pretext to call in the Geneva Convention troops.

Oddly enough, for the last several days Uwe's work had been relatively tranquil. The mass suicides and the declaration and the possible second coming of the Maelstrom had kept the people who were responsible for sending him multi-gigabyte reports detailing their specific demands busy—either killing someone or hiding in their houses or summer cottages.

"Uwe? Duty calls."

The Helix Inspection Agency office within the Chechnya Armistice Monitoring Group camp had been built in the ruins of an old city hall. I pressed my finger to the door to give my ID and let myself in. Uwe was asleep at his desk amid a mountain of printouts.

"Wakey, wakey," I said, giving him a slap on the back.

He blinked and looked befuddled for a second before his WatchMe kicked in and stimulated him to full alert mode. "Oh, hey, Tuan. Heard you were coming from Prime. She didn't deign to tell me why, though."

"Quite the office you got here. Isn't all this paper a fire hazard?"

"Meh. ThingList + NoTime = WhyClean?"

"Another victim of ThingList, huh? That seems to be going around."

Uwe shrugged his shoulders and cleared a teetering pile of papers from his desk onto the floor with a sigh.

"Have you been briefed on my current strategic action?"

Uwe raised an eyebrow. "Strategic action? I heard you were leading a one-woman idiot brigade, Miss Senior Inspector Tuan Kirie."

"Well let's make it two idiots then. I need your help."

"Let me guess. This has something to do with the six thousand suicides and the enforced murder dictate," Uwe said, though his expression told me that he really didn't know why I was here.

"That's right. You're familiar with the Anti-Russian Freedom Front?"

"Very. I arrange police protection for their negotiations—we've had a few with them already. Been trying to get them to agree to a lifestyle survey. They're one of Russia's top worries, but those of us wearing this symbol have to at least pretend to be neutral parties." He tapped the entwined serpents around the staff on his shirt.

"What makes them a top worry?"

"They're real good at moving around through the mountains. Guerrilla warfare at its finest. With all the cliffs and ravines up there, you can't even get a WarDog or WarDoll into play, so surrogate combat is completely out. Russia's been hiring every military resource supplier they can find to hit them where it hurts…and every single one has come running back down the mountain with their tails between their legs. What they really need is an elite squad—which the Russian national army has, but they're very reluctant to put actual soldiers into combat situations. I mean, hey, they might *die for real.* Not very popular with the folks back home. *We spend all this tax money on robots, so why do you go sending people in to die?* That sort of thing. It's a waste of human resources, and all that."

So Russia had gotten her fingers burned by the Freedom Front, and most of their people were probably in Moscow and St. Petersburg anyway, trying to keep the recent chaos in check. This meant that troops would be light on the ground out here on the front lines. I couldn't have picked a better time to contact the resistance.

"You still have an open channel with the Freedom Front?" I asked, suddenly recalling Vashlov's face as he said those words with his dying breaths.

"'Course. That's my job, after all."

"I need to get in contact with them. Right now."

Uwe's eyes went from narrow with suspicion to wide open. *Boy he's easy to read.*

"You kidding? It's way too dangerous. Whenever we hold negotiations we have to set a meeting place days in advance and arrange for contracted security. It's not something that can happen right now or even forty-eight hours from now."

"I don't need protection. I have something to give to one of the leaders of the front. Something very, very small. I don't even have to meet them in person, just get it to someone who can get it to them. Don't tell me you can't even do that?"

Uwe scrunched down into his gelatin seat and began tapping one finger on his chin. My guess was he was worried less about how to pull off my request and more about whether or not I was worth the trouble.

"Know what Stauffenberg told me?" I said. It wasn't really my style, but if there was ever a time to pull rank, now was it. "She said the fate of the world was resting on my shoulders."

"For real?"

"Feel free to call her up on your HeadPhone."

"No thanks. I spend enough time trying to avoid her calls as it is."

Uwe turned to look me straight in the eye and smiled. I detected a glimmer of irony. "This must be pretty serious for *you* to go pulling the Os Cara card."

"People are dying all over the world right now, and a lot more will be soon. If that's not serious enough, I don't know what is."

Uwe stretched in his chair and laughed out loud. The sound echoed off the walls of the spacious room. "No, no. I'm surprised *you* are serious about this, Tuan. I know your profile. I've heard the stories. Don't tell me you give a shit about what's going on in the world. You have some personal connection to this, don't you? That, and the thing with your dad—sorry about that, by the way. You don't strike me as the vengeful type, so I'm going to say you're after something. A little revenge on the side would just sweeten the deal. Look, I'm not one to point fingers. I'm here in this camp half for the booze and the smokes myself. As are the guys we got from your Niger operation. You're not the only one who wandered out here to get out of the kindness compactor and found themselves somehow responsible for the well-being of the whole fucking world."

I was shocked, a little, to find that there were others of like mind outside of the crew I had cultivated at my old post.

"You're working for yourself. Admit that, and I'll do what I can to help you."

I sighed, though to tell the truth I wasn't unhappy. I was starting to like this guy. "You might say it's a private affair."

"Private, eh? Sexy. I approve." Uwe's lips curled into a smile and his hand went to one ear to make a call. "Call the kid from the Fawn, will you? I doubt they have much business these days anyway. Right. Later."

≡

The Fawn was an eatery across the street from the old city hall where the camp was located. Much to my surprise, they had beer on the menu. Previously, their clientele had been mostly city officials. Portraits of several soldiers had been printed out and hung on the walls—memories of numerous conflicts this land had seen. I asked about them and Uwe chuckled.

"Those aren't printouts, Tuan. They're called photographs."

"Photographs?"

"Yeah. Bitch to make. You need all this film and photo paper and developing fluid. Really annoying protocol. It's not like just changing the cartridge in your printer."

"Another dead medium, then."

"Guilty as charged. Though for dead media, it's still pretty alive in these parts."

"Speaking of things I thought were dead and gone, I'm a little surprised they've got beer on the menu."

"Yeah. That's the kind of thing the Russians love to grumble about," Uwe said with a grin. "I can't tell you how many thousands of reports I've read about the 'shocking consumption of dangerous libations in this hopelessly backward region.'"

"I can imagine."

"Funny thing is, I looked into it and it turns out that out of all the thousands of admedistrations in the world, only twenty-six have laws on the books actually prohibiting alcohol. Just twenty-six that forbid their members to imbibe. In all the rest, it's just not done."

"I'm sure the SA analysts have something to do with that."

"Oh, I know. That's how the social assessment points work. As long as enough people agree about something, it starts being reflected in your points, and before you know it, you'd better behave or else. And enforcement is built in."

I smiled. "You know, I think this could be the start of a beautiful friendship."

"How nice of you to say that. I wouldn't mind—ah, here comes the food."

We were alone in the restaurant. The proprietor brought out our food on a large platter, placing it on our table before retreating to the kitchen.

"You think he's wondering what he should do before the deadline?" I asked, eyeing the retreating man.

"I doubt it. I certainly haven't given it any thought."

"That so?"

"You can believe me or not, makes no difference to me. I plan on taking whatever happens that day as it comes. More importantly, this here's a Chechen specialty. *Zhizhig galnash*. In other words, meat."

It was, literally, a mound of meat on a bed of what looked like penne. I dug in, the stench of mutton filling my nose. "You dip it in this," Uwe said, pushing a saucer of garlic oil across the table. It did a lot to improve the flavor. Still, the meat was unbelievably tough. I really had to go at it with fork and knife for a while before I made any progress.

The dishes kept coming out. There were lamb dumplings. And then more lamb. Eager to wash the taste out of my mouth, I found myself ordering a beer—right in front of a fellow Helix agent.

"Good call. I'll have one too. Don't see anyone else coming in tonight anyway."

"How do fool your WatchMe?"

"Ah, turns out that by agency regulations, the health risks associated with any consumption of alcohol during negotiations in regions where drinking is common isn't counted in your SA score. All I have to do is write a report. You went the DummyMe route, am I right? My way involves a little paperwork, but you got to hand it to the agency for showing a little common sense now and then."

"I had no idea."

"Few people do. Myself, I prefer to enjoy life, so I spend a lot of time finding loopholes in the system."

The proprietor brought out chicken pilaf next. I looked up from my plate to see a boy tapping Uwe on the shoulder. When did he get in here, I wondered. He certainly hadn't come in through the front door. He was wearing a necklace of spent rifle cartridges over a woven ethnic shawl of some sort. Maybe a warrior, and a young one at that. Uwe turned around and said something to him, upon which the boy faced me and stuck out his hand.

"He says give him whatever it is you have for his boss," Uwe explained.

I pulled a scrap of paper out of my pocket.

"What, just a piece of paper?" Uwe asked, and I assured him that was all. I told the boy to make sure his boss got it, and Uwe translated for me. The boy nodded, a serious look on his face, and slipped out through the back door of the bar.

"You sure that was all you wanted to give him?"

"I am. Better dig in. Your pilaf's getting cold."

"Not a bad idea—and since we're both here on business, we don't have to worry about oil or cholesterol or any moral concerns. Let's eat!"

≡

We stuffed ourselves and went back to Uwe's office, where he found a single folded piece of paper sitting on his desk. He frowned. "You got a response. That was quick."

I stepped in front of him and picked up the piece of paper. It began with a line of numbers: coordinates. And then a single word. ALONE.

"That's waaay out in the mountains," Uwe said.

I called up WorldVision in my AR and inputted the numbers. A visualization of the world appeared spinning in front of me until I was looking at Eurasia, then the line of the Caucasus in between the Black and Caspian seas. When the texture of the mountainsides became clear, I found I was looking at a rock-strewn hillside with a few straight lines defining the edges of something rectangular in the middle of it.

"That's a bunker. Pretty old by the looks of it. Must've been some Russians holed up to get away from the bombs last century or at the beginning of this one."

"I'm going. Think you can get me part of the way there?"

"By yourself? No way."

"I noticed your six-legger out front is armored."

"Yeah, it's got a cannon. I forget how many millimeters. That's an armed transport-use coolie goat."

"Then I'll need two days worth of food in bags on that thing. If you can get a truck to carry me and the goat as far as the road goes, that'll be fine."

"What about contracted security?"

"Won't need it."

"Then you'll be taking a one-way trip. I can't stand by and watch you do that."

Uwe was a surprisingly considerate man. I clapped him on the shoulder. "You wanted me to admit it, so here goes. This is a very personal mission for me. An extremely private mission."

"We're talking about your life here. I don't care how private your reasons are."

"No, we're talking about the life of every admedistration civilian in the world. Compared to that, I'm nothing at all. Remember what Stauffenberg said, the fate of the world is on my shoulders.

This is something I need to pull off on my own."

Uwe stared at me for a moment, not really buying my story. Then, at last, he shrugged. "You really do think about nothing other than yourself, do you?"

"That's right. Like you said, I'm very serious about this. And yeah, I don't give a shit what happens to the world."

"That's not very constructive of you, but I can't say I disapprove. Hey, I'm mostly in this job for the beer and the smokes myself."

Uwe put a hand to his ear and began talking to someone.

"Yuri? Hello? Uwe here. I need someone to carry a woman and a transport goat up into the mountains. Yeah, right away."

03

I could feel the wind growing colder against my skin with every gain in elevation.

It was just me and the six-legged goat in the back of the truck. The goat had been put together to army specs, so no pink was involved. Everything was drab olive, smoky, dirty—the colors of war. I had been told that the six-legger's control mechanism consisted of cultivated horse nerves specially trained for the environment. The original horse came from local stock, so they were used to the mountains, Uwe said. It bore a Geneva Convention Forces stencil on its amply armored side. There were cultivated parts, muscles extracted from an actual mountain goat, and a complex network of machinery, making it impossible to tell whether it was more biological or mechanical.

The goat had no head, and it would have taken considerable imagination to call the sensors bristling from its front end a face. The closest I could get to making sense of it was to think of it as a mountain goat with its head lopped off.

We went rocking and swaying up the mountain road for some time, but not once did the driver look back to talk to me. Not that I would have been able to respond, not knowing Russian. I was beginning to feel a strange affinity for my cybernetic companion when the truck came to a lurching stop.

The back opened, and the driver was standing outside, motioning me to exit. I gave the goat a slap on the rump and it stood smoothly under its heavy load and hopped down onto the gravelly path. I scanned an aerial photograph of our surroundings linked to the GPS in my AR. It would take a half day or more from here to reach the bunker site. There was hardly a path at all, but my high-resolution satellite imagery would make the going relatively painless. I waved to the driver and thanked him. He went back down the road without a word.

I was now thoroughly in the mountains. The rocky face of the Caucasus was black. According to Uwe, the name came from a Greek mutation of an ancient Scythian word meaning "white snow." Chechnya was to the north of the mountains, and our truck was now near the top of the range, close to the Georgian border to the south. The only snow on the Caucasus was at the peaks. Below 2,500 meters there was only black rock and dirt.

I started to navigate my way up the rocky slope, the goat deftly picking its way along behind me. I felt like a mountain ascetic on his way to meet the gods, though as soon as I had the thought, I banished it from my mind. I didn't think of—I didn't want to think of—Miach as a god.

There were no clouds. The humidity was low, but the sun didn't feel too hot as of yet. Despite the lack of a path, this was where the Chechen guerrillas had made their home, and I didn't find the going terribly difficult. I could feel the air in my lungs growing thinner as I climbed. A lack of oxygen wasn't something even WatchMe and a subdermal medcare unit could fix. I had gone off-line some time ago for that matter. My AR was a local simulation, working off the GPS I carried.

"Being this alone is actually kind of exciting," I said to the goat.

The goat plodded along in silence.

After three hours in the trackless wilderness, I found something resembling a proper path. According to my navigator, I had another six hours of this before I reached my destination. The path was fairly wide—I even saw traces of tire tracks. Probably left by the Russians during earlier conflicts in the region.

Every once in a while I rested to fill my mouth with water and acclimatize to the air. The transport goat had its own recycler unit embedded, so it didn't require much in the way of drink. I touched his back, as though it were a pet. It wasn't all that different from a regular animal. The skin was warm beneath a layer of fur. I had seen a civilian militia charge an army riding on these once, though I had forgotten whether it was in Niger or some other part of Africa.

The army in that conflict had been comprised entirely of remote surrogates. The militia had set off an electromagnetic pulse in the area, cutting the connection between the command center and the surrogates and forcing them to enter automated battle mode. Faced with a completely unexpected cybernetic cavalry charge, the surrogate troops had been decimated.

My goat was a slightly different beast than the ones they had ridden on, mine having been specially engineered for transporting goods in these mountains. The machine gun turret had been added on almost as an afterthought, and frankly I didn't really see the point. I stood, returned my canteen to its sack on the goat's back, checked the pistol in the holster at my side, and resumed my ascent.

Climb. Rest. Climb. Rest. Even as I grew used to the air, I could feel my stamina failing. This was a natural sensation that came with a reduction in oxygen—a physical symptom that my internal medcare plant couldn't hide by tweaking my nervous system as it did with pain and other discomfort. Proof that I was alive.

As history marched on, the range of natural experiences considered acceptable in life had shrunk. Where, I wondered, does one draw the line? Why form a wall around the soul or human consciousness? We had already conquered most natural diseases.

We had elevated the myth of a normalized human body to a high public standard.

My thoughts drifted while I climbed.

Take diabetes, for example. In its original form, diabetes was a feature humans had developed that helped to deal with cold climates. Water with glucose has a freezing point below zero—beneficial for people faced with the sudden onset of cold temperatures. Even if the sugar destroyed your veins and your kidneys, you'd still live a decade or two, and if you managed to reproduce during that time it was a big win for your DNA. Diabetes was a vital part of our slipshod evolution.

Qualities that were vital in some circumstances became useless or even dangerous when those circumstances changed. We are just collections of DNA optimized for particular places and times. The human genome was a patchwork of solutions for a thousand different problems. It was easy to think of evolution as meaning forward progress, when in reality we, and all living things, were just assorted attempts at survival.

So why put human consciousness up on the altar? Why worship this strange artifact we had attained? Morality, holiness—these were just things our brains picked up along the way, pieces of the patchwork. We only experienced sadness and joy because they benefited our survival in a particular environment. That said, I couldn't understand how something like joy was really vital. Nor did I know why sadness and despair had helped us survive.

Still, like diabetes, what if the useful shelf life of our emotions had expired some time ago? What if an environment that required us to feel emotions and possess a consciousness was gone? Why hesitate to cure our brains of emotions and consciousness like we had cured our bodies of diabetes?

Mankind had once required anger.

Mankind had once required joy.

Mankind had once required sadness.

Mankind had once required happiness.

Once, once, once.

My epitaph for an environment, and an age, that had disappeared.

Mankind had once required the belief that "I" was "I."

Keita Saeki, Gabrielle Étaín, and Nuada Kirie.

My encounters with them had removed any basis I had felt for "me" to exist. Like what my father had said about people with the recessive gene for deafness coupling in Martha's Vineyard, here people with the recessive gene for the absence of consciousness coupled, and *that* was normal.

Maybe as long as a society based on mutual aid was in place, outmoded features like consciousness were fated to disappear. Maybe we should embrace the social systems we'd developed and throw out the spawning pool of opposition, hesitation, and anguish that was consciousness altogether.

Where are the whys that drive me located?

Where are the words that protect my soul?

Wasn't my desire to avenge Cian Reikado and my father's death just the vestiges of a once-vital but now derelict function of my obsolete simian midbrain?

In the past, it was religion that guaranteed "I" was "I." Everything had been laid out by God, so it wasn't our place to question things. Now society had entirely lost the functions that religion once performed. Because once we accepted that emotions and all other phenomena occurring in the brain were just traits that happened to be beneficial to our survival at some point in the past, most ideas of morality lost their absolute basis. A morality without absolute conviction—an objective morality—was weak. History contained ample proof of this.

At any rate, today I was going to meet Miach Mihie.

I expected she would have some answers to all this.

After several more breaks, I reached the bunker just as the sun was slipping below the jagged horizon. I could see clouds gathering far off in the distance, and I wondered what elevation I had reached.

One corner of the bunker jutted out from the mountain face,

a smooth panel of concrete against the rough edges of rock, with an open doorway in its center.

"Wait here, goaty."

I used my fingerprint to lock the goat's weapon systems and checked my own sidearm.

```
<list:protocol>
     <p: Check the spring on the magazine.>
     <p: Remove and reinsert the rounds.>
     <p: Pull back the slide until it locks, then:>
     <p: Check if there are any rounds in the
     chamber.>
     <p: Carefully check the action of all other
     parts, depending on the type of firearm.>
</list>
```

"Okay. I can do this," I muttered to myself, stepping into the reinforced concrete bunker dug into the mountainside.

"Hello there, Tuan. How long has it been, thirteen years?" came a voice from the darkness inside. The only sounds were the dripping of water and the scuffing of my feet on the ground. I pulled my gun from its holster, the sound of my clothes rubbing together loud in my ears.

"You won't need your gun. We're the only ones here, Tuan. Just me and you."

One step.

Then another.

I switched my AR to light-enhancement mode, revealing the interior of the dimly lit bunker.

"I knew you'd come. I knew you were the only one who'd come."

I had left the entrance behind me now, where the goat patiently awaited my return.

"I'm right over here, Tuan."

Miach Mihie appeared as if out of thin air, right in front of the raised barrel of my gun.

She looked almost the same as she had the last time I saw her, when we had been little girls.

"It was a nice idea, bringing my business card. The one I gave you back in high school. I knew it was you right away," Miach said, raising the card I'd brought from my desk back in Japan. The one I had handed to the messenger boy at the Fawn.

"I knew you would," I said, keeping the barrel pointed at her. "Vashlov told me you were here."

"I'm sorry about Vashlov, and about your father."

Strangely enough, hearing it from Miach didn't make the blood rush to my head, though I could feel the rage simmering down inside somewhere along with my memories of Cian Reikado.

"I was sure you'd say it couldn't be helped."

"Okay, I will. It couldn't be helped."

I pulled the trigger. The bullet scraped Miach's white cheek, leaving a single red line to mark its path.

"Not from where I'm standing. No one had to die."

"I can see that," she said. "And I hope no one else has to leave this world."

"Roughly six thousand people attempted to commit suicide, and of them, nearly three thousand were successful. All lifeist society has been plunged into a murderous mayhem by your one-person, one-kill declaration. And you hope no one else has to die?"

"We had to do all that, otherwise the old geezers wouldn't push the button."

"Wouldn't push the—"

And then it was all clear to me.

I knew what Miach was thinking.

I knew exactly what scenario Miach had painted for the world. I stood with my mouth hanging open, gun still pointed at her.

"That's right, Tuan," she said. "We want Harmony."

04

<recollection>
It was the day we took those pills.

"I'm taking those things that gave me strength along with me," Miach said.

I had gotten a call from her and come out to the river just as the sun was beginning to set that night. She was pouring gasoline from a plastic container onto a massive pile of books lying on the riverbank. I have no idea how she'd managed to get them all there. I asked her what she was doing, realizing as I did what an obvious question it was, and yet also feeling that it was my expected role to ask regardless.

"I'm going to burn them. Every one of them."

If that were true, then the pile of books here represented her entire library, painstakingly compiled over years of allowance. I'd never been to her house at that point, so I had no way of knowing whether these were all of her books. Yet it seemed unlikely that Miach would lie about it.

"I don't think I could go with these still here."

"Go where?"

Miach waved her hand at our surroundings, no, at the entire world. "To the other side, away from here. To the place people call heaven or hell. To nothing. I'm afraid these little ones would hold me back, keep me bound here. Besides, if I waited any longer, I'd be too weak to carry them."

Miach emptied the last drop from the plastic tank she carried. She looked inside and made a face, then pointed the tank mouth toward me.

"Ugh. Gasoline smells terrible. Want a whiff?"

I respectfully declined.

"When a new emperor came into power in China, they would burn all the history books. So they could write new histories," Miach told me as she screwed the cap back on.

I nodded appreciatively, enjoying the feeling of *agreeing* with her. Whenever I did that, it felt like Miach was recording a little bit of herself onto me.

"Then, at some point, the whole world became a giant book," Miach said. People thought they could record everything, so they did.

The advent of the CAT scan changed the world.

X-rays were just photographs, but CAT scans were X-rays taken from multiple angles, combined into images by formulas applied by computers before being output in a visual manner. A photograph was a representation, but a CAT scan was a record.

"You think WatchMe is like a part of that?" I asked.

Miach pulled some matches from a pocket and nodded. "It's the ultimate form of body-recording."

Our bodies were being replaced by a record, and it all began with a CAT scan. Whatever happened next would be only a matter of degree. It was constant, and it was already happening. That was what WatchMe was intended to achieve. "That's why I want to die as a little girl, before I put that thing in my body, before I become something that's read, like a book."

To prove that these tits, this ass, this belly, aren't a book.

"Why do you think people write things?"

I shrugged.

"Because words remain. Maybe for an eternity. Or at least for something approaching that. The Bible was written for that matter. And the pyramids are kind of a record too."

People had always been obsessed with the idea of eternity. No other age had ever convinced more people that their bodies were eternal things. Old age still hung on, a weak, nearly silenced cry of nature, that would doubtlessly soon be conquered. Barbarism had been conquered. "Maybe the Maelstrom was a form of rehabilitation, returning the balance of things to their natural state," Miach said with a sigh.

Miach walked over to where I stood behind her, watching.

"What?" I said, and she pressed the matches into my right hand and closed my fingers around them. Her cool hands felt good against my skin.

"Could you do this for me? I made it this far, but I don't think I can do the rest."

"Okay," I said.

Like an athlete lighting a sacred flame, I solemnly tossed a match onto the pile of books. The fire caught in an instant, reducing the pile to ash in a matter of moments. The setting sun painted the riverbank with strange light, while the plasma glow of the fire lit us up from below.

"They used to burn bodies like this in Japan."

"Really?"

"Of course, that all changed with the Maelstrom." Miach smiled. Everything had changed. After the great chaos came the great control. And that hardened so fast it could never be shaken.

"They called it cremation. They would put the things the person loved in their life inside the coffin with them. That custom ended when they started liquefying bodies."

"Is this your cremation, Miach?" I asked.

"Yeah," she said. "Because they won't put these books in my coffin. They gave me strength, so I'm taking them with me."

We stood there for a long time, until the sun had set, and Miach's books had burned out and Miach's cremation was over. Then we sat on the riverbank and looked out at the town. Miach appointed names for the buildings with one finger, saying, "That's eternity. That's the castle of people who believe themselves to be eternal. There's the king. There's the government. Those are the old names for the stronghold of rule that the admedistrations have divided into tiny little pieces.

"I want to kick their eternity in the shins. Catch it with a sucker punch.

"I want to hit their frozen time where it hurts."

"Is that what our deaths will be?" I asked. "Will the world change?"

"Everything will, for us," Miach replied.

```
</recollection>
```

"We've come all this way," Miach said, and she danced a little jig in one spot. *Tap tap tap*. She was a little taller, and her tits were more substantial than mine. But she was still a cute little girl.

"What do you mean, 'all this way'?"

"To a brave new world."

I had no idea what she was talking about.

"I'm talking about a utopia, Tuan Kirie. A World State. Like in Aldous Huxley's book."

Tap tap.

"Will we strive for paradise, or will we strive for the truth? After the Maelstrom, mankind chose paradise. We chose a false eternity; we chose to deny that we are nothing more than a collection of adaptation patches applied via the evolutionary process to fit this or that situation. We could have it, if only we could suppress nature. If we could make everything around us artificial, it could be ours. And we've already crossed the point of no return."

I frowned, still holding up my gun.

Wasn't it you who hated that world? Wasn't it you who denied it? You, Miach Mihie?

Ta-ta-tap.

"My father told me that you were—"

"That's right, a person without a consciousness. Or you might say, someone who doesn't require a consciousness. I should say I *was* a person without a consciousness, now that I've gone and gotten myself one. It was born here."

Miach spread her arms and twirled like a ballerina, showing me the concrete cave.

Phweew, phweew, phweew.

The wind whipping across the heights of the Caucasus made a sad sound like a flute as it passed through the opening to the bunker.

Phweew, phweew, phweew.

"This was the base of operations for the Russian army's prostitution ring. The girls they caught on the battlefield were raped here by the Russian soldiers every day."

Phweew, phweew.

"One of the generals who raped me used to make me touch his antique Tokarev while he penetrated me again and again. This is a gun, he'd say, this is steel, this is power—like it was his second penis. He would stick it in my mouth and make me suck it, over and over and over."

I was already crying.

And wondering what sort of consciousness it took to think about such things and say them so calmly, so brightly.

Phweew, phweew, phweew.

I put a hand to my mouth, holding back a wave of nausea.

"I had the gun in my mouth, was covering it with my own saliva, when my consciousness awoke. This concrete cave is filled with juices—semen, vaginal secretions, blood, tears, snot, and sweat. In that liquid I was born again."

Ta-tap, ta-tap, ta-tap.

"In the end, some vigilantes and an MRS the Chechens had hired saved me. I was picked up by a Japanese adoption agency program seeking to counter the declining population problem, and came to Japan."

"You told me," I managed to say, my eyes and nose running. At some point I had lost the ability to keep my emotions dammed up inside me. "You told me you hated this world. The world of love-and-be-loved that tried to strangle you with kindness. But was it really so bad? Was it worse than Chechnya? Was our society a more terrible place than this bunker?"

"I didn't know what to do," Miach said.

Ta-ta-tap.

"When I was twelve years old, the boy living next door to me hanged himself."

Ta-ta-tap, ta-ta-tap, ta-ta-tap.

"He said he hated this world, that he didn't belong here, and he died. I thought about that. I knew how barbaric people could be. And I knew how broken they could become when they tried to repress that nature. I thought that this society, admedistrative society, this lifeist system was all wrong. A society that wanted me to regulate myself internally, even while people were killing themselves all around me, was just bizarre."

It was true that Miach's passion had given me and Cian a different view of the world and of a society based on the constant monitoring of the human body and health as a value above all others. A society where rigid self-monitoring was the only path to peace and harmony.

"That's right, you hated the system of the world. That's why when you asked us to die, me and Cian said yes."

Something about the way I was speaking reminded me of how I talked back in high school. Like when I had been a little girl, eating my lunch with Miach Mihie and Cian Reikado.

"But I learned something when I left with your father, Tuan."

"What?"

"That people can change. If people can break through the barrier of consciousness."

Ta-ta-tap tap. Ta-ta-tap tap.

"So you didn't cultivate this chaos because you hate the world," I said, lowering my gun at last.

Miach continued her dance for an audience of one. "That's right. I love it. I love it with all my being—and I want to affirm it. I want to cure the world of its infection, its 'me's and 'I's." Miach looked serious. Her dance quickened. "I wrote most of the source code for the neural network your father and his friends installed into the midbrain of every WatchMe user in the world. There were backdoors in the WatchMe control systems of several admedistrations. Backdoors left for us. With such access, it was easy to create a hyperbolic desire for death in many people."

All they had to do was reset the value of death as greater than the person's will for life for the victim to choose oblivion. For those people who quite suddenly found death to be irresistibly attractive, a choice to make, there was no avoiding the erroneous value system's effect.

"But the old folks got scared."

"The ones running the Next-Gen group."

"Yes, and your father was the ideologue at their center."

"Ah yes. His proclamation that the creation of a perfect person for our society would make the soul a useless artifact. Funny, isn't it?"

"I wasn't laughing." Miach stopped her dance and brought her hands together with a loud clap. I heard echoes run through the dark bunker. "I realized that's what we had to do. There are tens of thousands of girls and boys killing themselves in the world right now. Adults too. We can never remove the barbarism of nature from ourselves completely. We can't forget that before we are little admedistrative collectives, before we are part of a system or network of relationships, we are animals, plain and simple—a patchwork assortment of functions and logic and emotion all tied together into a bundle."

"So you thought that if people were dying because they couldn't get used to this world—"

"Yes. That we should give up being human in the first place."

Ta-tap, ta-tap, ta-tap.

Miach resumed her light dance. "By which I mean, we should give up being conscious. We should give up our roughshod armor and become part of the society gnawing at our bones. We should give up being ourselves. Get rid of 'me' and consciousness and everything else our environment foisted on us. Only then can our society reach the harmony it was striving for."

Ta-ta-ta-ta-tap, ta-tap, ta-tap-ta.

"They used to tell soldiers they weren't supposed to wear

boots to fit their bodies, they were supposed to fit their bodies into their boots. And we can do that, easily."

"If the old folks would agree with you."

Once again, Miach's dance ceased. She let her shoulders fall with a sigh. "That's right. The old folks think the end of consciousness is a kind of death. Even though there had been a minority living in the Caucasus mountains for thousands of years without anything like a consciousness. As long as a mature system is in place, there is no need for conscious decisions. We have a sufficiently mutually beneficial system, we have software to tell us how to live, we've outsourced everything possible, so what need have we of consciousness? The problem isn't our consciousness, it's the pain that our having a consciousness brings us when we are forced to regulate ourselves for health or for the community."

"We don't need a will, we don't need consciousness. And how does this connect with the chaos in the world now?"

"It's easy. If the world is teetering on the brink of destruction, the old folks will have no choice but to press the button."

Of course. It was so simple.

"So you're pushing them to a place where they'll have to take our consciousnesses away?"

"That's right."

"You've engineered this whole situation, then?"

"That's right. Technically speaking, it's not an actual button. It's a series of codes."

Codes. A string of letters telling the world to be a certain way.

That the world is so.

"We tried to grab that authority ourselves but were unable to. That's when the split in the Next-Gen group happened. The main group believes that the reflective consciousness, the part that says 'I am me,' must be respected as a vital part of humanity. The minority group, which is us, believe that in our perfected social system, only the human brain remains, and consciousness is only good for unhappiness and should be swept away. They called us heretics, which is why I had to run away, back to the

Chechens who had saved me before."

Miach and her cohorts had used the authority they had to the fullest.

They had infiltrated several admedistration servers to which they had access and were able to directly change the value system lodged in the midbrains of constituents. Yet the old guard, despite their memories of the Maelstrom, and ironically the ones who still revered the soul, retained a firm grip on the power of human consciousness. And according to Miach, it had been my dad who held the line with the most determination of all.

I remembered that day when I was eight or nine when that woman in the session chewed out my dad about caffeine. He had folded before her then, his self-respect melting like ice cream on a summer day, but here, he had believed in the human soul, and consciousness, and the existence of "me" till the end.

I felt myself growing sad. Sad about how my father had died. This was more than enough reason to want to avenge him.

"Your father was veeery stubborn," Miach said, smiling and pointing at me. "He saw the hundreds of thousands of people dying in the worst way possible—suicide—and he pitied them, yet he still claimed we needed our human wills, our consciousnesses. I disagreed. I felt like I had to do something. I wanted to make a world with no souls, for the sake of the hundreds of thousands of souls we lose every year."

Phweew, phweew, phwee, phweew.
Phweew, phweew, phweew.

The wind blew through the bunker past where we were standing.

I raised my gun again, letting the front sight straight at Miach's heart, the barrel pointed toward Miach.

"Cian died. My father died. You killed them."

Miach nodded, her face severe. "I had to. Note that they were randomly selected from all potential targets."

"My father's death wasn't random."

"That's true. Your father died for his beliefs." She pointed at the gun in my hand. "What about you, Tuan Kirie?"

I listened to my own voice speaking inside me. Would this voice go away if I lost my consciousness, my will? Would my consciousness, my individuality, disperse, leaving only a system behind? Leaving only a self-evident me? Would I do what I was supposed to do, never wondering, always working, my various functions all handled automatically?

The harmonious brain is a brain with all uncertainty removed. No, discarded.

With no uncertainty, there were no choices. With no choices, everything simply was.

I understood that everything around me would look exactly the way it always had. If human consciousness had never done anything of great importance, its loss would change little.

People go shopping, just like they did the day before.

People go to work, just as they had the day before.

People would laugh like they did the day before.

People would cry like they did the day before.

All reactions would be clear and simple. Doing things because they were what you were supposed to do.

Wasn't this just some rite of passage we all had to go through in order to create the coming eternity?

I thought that maybe it was.

No objections.

≡

"So you wanted to go back to your life without a consciousness. To the way your people used to be."

Miach looked down, then nodded slightly. "Maybe that's true. Yes, I think you're right."

"So by taking that away, maybe I can have my revenge."

"Huh?"

Miach blinked. Revenge? It was like she hadn't even once

considered the idea the whole time I was making my way to her hiding place, carrying Cian's and my father's deaths with me.

It was enough to make me want to laugh. She was Miach Mihie all right, this girl. Oddly enough, it was a relief.

Say, Miach. You know how many times I've thought about killing you between the moment Cian Reikado's face hit her *caprese* and when I found my way to your bunker in Chechnya?

"Cian didn't have to die. That's why you called her to tell her she had to."

"You think?"

"You had to justify your own consciousness, vis-a-vis a reality that had already been decided and could not be stopped."

"I'm not so sure."

I nodded, steadying my grip on the gun. "That's why I'm going to avenge Cian and my father, right here."

"How?"

"I'm going to make the world you always wanted a reality. And I'm not going to let you be part of it."

Phweew, phweew, phweew.

I pulled the trigger.

Miach fell to the concrete floor with a thud.

A shrill rush of air spilled from her mouth, along with a tiny voice seemingly wrung from her body that said, "Will you forgive me now?"

"For Cian and my father?"

"Yeah."

"I've had my revenge."

I reached down and stroked Miach's hair where she lay. A single rivulet of red blood running from one corner of her mouth was beautiful against her white skin. Her eyes looked weakly down at the floor where those men had reveled in their barbarism.

"Please, take me with you."

"To where?"

"A place where...I can see the Caucasus."

Miach was bleeding from the two holes my bullets had left in her chest.

One for Cian.

One for my father.

I threw her over my shoulder and walked through the bunker. It was just like Miach always said. Like Uwe said. I didn't care what happened to the world. No matter what the mobs crushing down on the pink-camouflaged soldiers and their useless nonlethal weapons were going to do. No matter how men with knives cut at each other. No matter if the old folks entered the final code to stop it all.

I brought Miach out to the corner of the bunker where it stuck out over the side of the mountain like a stage. Snow came drifting in through the open entranceway.

White snow on the black mountains.

I saw them stretching off into the distance, their crowns capped with ice.

"Will you stay and watch?"

"Watch what?"

"Watch my consciousness end."

I nodded.

I had fired the bullets. They were fired by no one else's will but mine.

I did it. I did it.

Me.

The last white puff of breath came from Miach Mihie's mouth.

Her body, her brain, lost their warmth, and her consciousness—that which made her Miach—faded, thanks to that simple, ancient mechanism known as death. It didn't make a difference that her consciousness had been an emulation in her cerebrum.

I stood in the whirling snow that came inside the bunker for a moment.

The sound of a drop of blood falling from Miach's spent shell brought me back to my senses.

"It's cold here," I said to the backdrop of the mountains, holding Miach in my arms.

I felt a cold creep across my cheeks.

I wondered where my body ended and the cold air began.

The boundary was already vague in my mind.

Phweew, phweew, phweew, phweew.
Goodbye, me.

Good
bye,
m—

```
</body>
</etml>
```

<null>
me
</null>

<part:number=epilogue:title=In This Twilight/>

```
<?Emotion-in-Text Markup Language:version=1.2:enc
oding=EMO-590378?>
<!DOCTYPE etml PUBLIC :-//WENC//DTD ETML 1.2
transitional//EN>
//<etml:lang=jp>
<etml:lang=en>
<body>
```

This is the last day of human consciousness.
The day that several billion "me"s ceased to exist.
This text is a story written from the viewpoint of one of the *Homo sapiens* involved with these events.

This text has been tagged with etml 1.2. If you have compatible emotional textures installed in your texture reader, you will be able to reenact all of the emotions referred to in the text, as well as experience meta-functions at certain points as you make your way through. At present, the etml embedded in this text serves only as a trigger for you to reproduce the various emotional functions left behind in the brain. As humanity is perfectly socialized at present, there are few situations that call for any great display of emotion, either positive or negative.

≡

Let me tell you about what happened after the Caucasus.
Shortly after Tuan made her way down the mountain, the old folks decided to destroy consciousness and thereby equalize

all members of society at once. Those elders with the authority
went to their own rooms and entered their fragments of the code
into their terminals. At that moment, the angels took up the
hymn of Harmony and spread their wings before every person
with WatchMe installed, all over the world.

When the angels' wings touched the peoples' heads, their
consciousness and wills were gone.

In this new world, everything was self-evident, with nothing
left to be chosen.

We are alive.

In a world where everything is as it should be.

No wondering, no choices, no decisions. Something very close
to heaven.

```
<music:name=Messiah:id=2yr6r58jnjhu7451110e99>
     <Hallelujah!>
     <Hallelujah!>
     <Hallelujah!>
     <Hallelujah!>
     <Hallelujah!>
</music>
```

The riots stopped immediately.

As though they had suddenly remembered what they were
doing, everyone went back to their roles within the social system.
The several billion people in the world with WatchMe installed
had ceased being animals.

We finally arrived at the perfect social existence we had been
heading toward in fits and starts since antiquity.

It was then that the sociology and economics studies of the
previous age, when mankind had been partially animal, fell apart
in the course of a night. When a perfectly purified and adapted
man became the smallest unit of a social existence, sociology
and economics transformed into pure logic.

On the surface, of course, nothing changed.

People cried as though they were sad and raged as though they were angry. But these actions carried the same value as the mimicked emotional responses a robot would have had in the previous era. All people had lost their inward minds.

Mankind was in perfect harmony with its medical industrial society.

The instant the old folks had entered their codes and the Harmony program had begun to sing, suicide disappeared from human society. Nearly all battles ceased. The individual was no longer a unit. The entire social system was the unit. By losing its sense of self and self-awareness, society had been freed from the pain it suffered because its systems had relied on imperfect humans, arriving for the first time at a perfect bliss.

I am a part of the system, as you are part of the system.
No one felt any pain about that any longer.
There was no "me" to feel pain.
I had been replaced by a single whole, by "society."

The age when consciousness had been a valued facet of humanity was long past.

Though it is hard to estimate now, the age when "I" and "consciousness" and "will" had played an important role in making decisions was not a short one. For modern man, in perfect accordance with the system, there is no need for icons such as those the *Homo sapiens* called gods and heroes, yet there can be no harm in learning about these things.

Once there were two women named Miach Mihie and Tuan Kirie.

They were the last to pay their respects to our "selves."

"Goodbye, me.
"Goodbye, soul.
"Though we may never meet again, goodbye."

Those are the last words Tuan whispered, just before her WatchMe went online and nonconsciousness fell upon her. Words to put at ease several billion souls about to be lost.

Is there is a heaven on this earth?

If mankind can truly ever touch something perfect.
This is probably the closest thing to heaven we, as vertebrates patched together from a long string of evolutionary changes, can hope to achieve. To climb the ladder to a place where the self and society become one.

Now, we are happy.

So

so

happy.

```
</body>
</etml>
```

ACKNOWLEDGEMENTS

With thanks to my parents and uncle and aunt, who
were there for me in my time of need.

ABOUT THE AUTHOR

Keikaku (Project) Itoh was born in Tokyo in 1974. He graduated from Musashino Art University. In 2007, he debuted with *Gyakusatsu Kikan* (Genocidal Organs) and took first prize in the "Best SF of 2007" in *SF Magazine*. He is also the author of *Metal Gear Solid: Guns of the Patriots*, a Japanese-language novel based on the popular video game series.

After a long battle with cancer, Itoh passed away in March 2009. Itoh revised *Harmony* while in the hospital receiving treatment for the disease.

HAIKASORU
THE FUTURE IS JAPANESE

HARMONY BY PROJECT ITOH

In the future, Utopia has finally been achieved thanks to medical nanotechnology and a powerful ethic of social welfare and mutual consideration. This perfect world isn't that perfect though, and three young girls stand up to totalitarian kindness and super-medicine by attempting suicide via starvation. It doesn't work, but one of the girls—Tuan Kirie—grows up to be a member of the World Health Organization. As a crisis threatens the harmony of the new world, Tuan rediscovers another member of her suicide pact, and together they must help save the planet…from itself.

ROCKET GIRLS BY HOUSUKE NOJIRI

Yukari Morita is a high school girl on a quest to find her missing father. While searching for him in the Solomon Islands, she receives the offer of a lifetime—she'll get the help she needs to find her father, and all she need do in return is become the world's youngest, lightest astronaut. Yukari and her teen friends, all petite, are the perfect crew and cargo for the Solomon Space Association's launches, or will be once they complete their rigorous and sometimes dangerous training.

THE OUROBOROS WAVE BY JYOUJI HAYASHI

Ninety years from now, a satellite detects a nearby black hole scientists dub Kali after the Hindu goddess of destruction. Humanity embarks on a generations-long project to tap the energy of the black hole and establish colonies on planets across the solar system. Earth and Mars and the moons Europa (Jupiter) and Titania (Uranus) develop radically different societies, with only Kali, that swirling vortex of destruction and creation, and the hated but crucial Artificial Accretion Disk Development association (AADD) in common.

SUMMER, FIREWORKS, AND MY CORPSE BY OTSUICHI

Two short novels, including the title story and *Black Fairy Tale*, plus a bonus short story. *Summer* is a simple story of a nine-year-old girl who dies while on summer vacation. While her youthful killers try to hide her body, she tells us the story—from the point of view of her dead body—of the boys' attempt to get away with murder. *Black Fairy Tale* is classic J-horror: a young girl loses an eye in an accident, but receives a transplant. Now she can see again, but what she sees out of her new left eye is the experiences and memories of its previous owner. Its previous *deceased* owner.

VISIT US AT WWW.HAIKASORU.COM